# Accounting Isn't Always Kosher

Habent Sua Fata Libelli

**ABSOLUTELY AMA*ING* eBOOKS**

Manhanset House
Shelter Island Hts., New York 11965-0342

bricktower@aol.com • tech@absolutelyamazingebooks.com
• absolutelyamazingebooks.com

The Absolutely Amazing eBooks colophon is a trademark of
J. T. Colby & Company, Inc.

**Library of Congress Cataloging-in-Publication Data**
McMillan, Steve
Accounting Isn't Always Kosher.
p. cm.

1. FICTION / Mystery & Detective / Amateur Sleuth.
2. FICTION / Mystery & Detective / General.
3. FICTION / Thrillers / Jewish.
Fiction, I. Title.
ISBN: 978-1-955036-42-9 Trade Paper

November 2022

# Accounting Isn't Always Kosher

Steve McMillan

# Accounting Mysteries

## By Steve McMillan

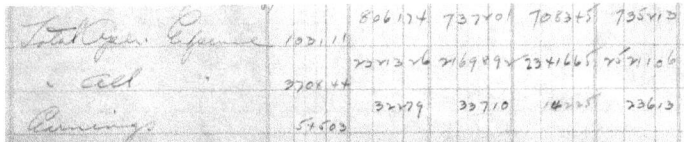

*Accounting Can Be Murder*
*Accounting And Murder Around The World*
*Accounting For Vampires*
*Accounting For Pirates*

**Available from**
**AbsolutelyAmazingEbooks.com**

# Table of Contents

# Acknowledgments

Thanks to Fran, Norah, Regina, and Susan.
Thanks to Shirrel, John, Terry, and Jane.
Thanks to Emily, Mikayla, Mike, Matt, and Liam.
And, as always, thanks to Debbi for being Debbi.

# Chapter One

Josef Goldstein sat very nervously in a chair across from the two Russian mobsters. He knew he was taking a big risk meeting with these two, but he didn't feel he had much choice. His daughter, Riva, had been trying to get divorced from her husband for many months, but Lev, Josef's son-in-law, had utterly refused to consider it. And according to ultra-Orthodox Jewish doctrine, if Lev didn't grant Riva a get, a Jewish divorce decree, the divorce couldn't happen. Josef had offered Lev money, part of his business, and even the house that he and Riva shared. But Lev was outraged that Riva wanted to divorce him and considered it a public embarrassment in front of their Orthodox community, so he steadfastly refused. Josef had asked their rabbi to intercede, but Lev had even refused the rabbi's request.

Josef had heard of mobsters in New York, particularly in the Crown Heights area in Queens, who would "encourage" Jewish men to sign the get so that their divorces would be considered religiously legal. Josef didn't know anyone in New York who could help, but a member of his shul had heard of a group of Russian Jewish mobsters in Northeast Philly who might be able to help. Josef had thought long and hard about getting involved with these guys, but he was running out of options, so he set up a meeting with Mikhail Rabinovich and Boris Reznick.

Rabinovich and Reznick had immigrated to the US from Russia ten years before. They had been involved with the Russian Mob back in St. Petersburg but had found there was too much competition in that city. They were making a decent living back in Russia, but they had found out from friends and relatives that the

US was very ripe for the picking. Initially, they had planned on New York, but, similar to St. Peterburg, there was too much competition, so they decided on Philadelphia. Since coming to Philly, they had done very well with money laundering, a little extortion, and running some drugs. But they were always looking for new opportunities, hence the meeting with Josef.

Rabinovich said, "So, Mr. Goldstein, how do you think we can be of service to you?"

Josef responded in a cracked voice, "As you probably figured out by my apparel, I adhere to ultra-Orthodox Judaism, as does all of my family. I'm assuming that you know what a get is." Both Rabinovich and Reznick nodded. "My daughter Riva would like to get divorced from her husband, but the jerk will not sign the get, so she can't be divorced according to Orthodox Jewish law."

Reznick asked, "So why does she want a divorce? Has her husband been cruel to her?"

"Not cruel in a physical sense: he doesn't hit her. But he is very psychologically cruel. He constantly berates her in front of people. He makes fun of her even at our shul. And they have two children, a boy and a girl, and he doesn't provide for them very well. Oh, they eat, but he could provide many other things for his kids, but he chooses not to. And he has a successful business in the Northeast, so it's not a question of money."

Rabinovich inquired, "What kind of business does he have?"

"He has a small jewelry store in a shopping center. He has contacts in Israel and Brussels from whom he buys small diamonds and other jewels. It's not a huge store, but he does pretty well."

Reznick asked, "Any idea how much he brings in each year?"

"Close to a $100,000, I would guess. He is not rich, but given the ultra-Orthodox lifestyle, he does okay. We live rather frugal lives."

Reznick asked, "So what would you like us to do? Shake down his business a little?"

Josef replied, "No, not that at all. I don't care about his business and money. I want him to sign the get for my daughter's divorce."

Reznick said, "So you want us to 'encourage' him to sign the document."

"Yes, I am willing to pay for your services. How much do you think I would need to pay?"

Reznick and Rabinovich looked at each other and smiled. Rabinovich said, "50 large, and we'll get you what you want."

Josef was a bit taken aback. He said, "$50 thousand is a lot of money. As I said, I'm not a rich man."

Reznick replied, "Well, that's the price. Take it or leave it. Totally up to you."

Josef pondered for a moment and said, "Okay, deal." He stuck out his hand to shake.

Before he reached for Josef's hand, Rabinovich said, "We'll need half up front and the rest when the task is complete."

Josef kept his hand out and nodded. He shook hands with both Rabinovich and Reznick. He felt like he had just cut a deal with the devil.

In fact, that's precisely what he had done!

# Chapter Two

It was just another typical day at Temple: teaching, advising, and doing a little research. But it was different because I spent some time with the Public Company Accounting Oversight Board. The PCAOB was established after the Enron scandal in the early 2000s to improve accounting firms' auditing. While Sharon and I were down at the Outer Banks, I had been approached to work with the PCAOB. I had not thought it was that big of a commitment, but I had been wrong so far. In the last couple of months, I had been given three Philadelphia accounting firms to examine for their compliance with standard auditing procedures.

The work was not that hard, but it was very time-consuming. I am very familiar with auditing procedures, even with large firms, so I knew what to look for, and the three firms I had been given were not that large. My job was to review their audit procedures, particularly their internal control processes, to ensure that the control systems were properly in place. The internal control process is critical when auditing even a medium-sized firm because it is tough and laborious to manually examine a firm's accounting activities, such as accounts receivable, accounts payable, and even sales. Adding up a firm's total sales, perhaps in the multi-million-dollar range, requires too much time and labor. So, the audit focuses on how a firm posts all of its transactions and the internal control procedures used to make it unlikely there is a misstatement of any accounting transactions.

The Enron scandal had shown that internal controls could be made to look legitimate and work correctly even if they aren't. Enron's finance and accounting personnel had fabricated fraudulent financial statements for years. One of their favorite ways to manipulate their earnings was using mark-to-market accounting. Basically, mark-to-market accounting allowed Enron to book tremendous sales numbers without having any actual cash actually exchanging hands. So, it looked like Enron was extremely successful on paper, but Enron was a house of cards. Enron executives were making millions of dollars, but the company was actually bleeding money at every turn. Enron went from a $65 billion company to bankruptcy in twenty-four days when the scandal finally broke. Twenty-two thousand people lost their jobs and savings. The largest and oldest public accounting firm, Arthur Andersen, went bankrupt, too. The PCAOB was created so that that type of financial meltdown would never happen again.

From what I know and have read about, the PCAOB has had some successes and failures. One of their biggest failures occurred with KPMG LLP in 2018. The Securities and Exchange Commission examiners found that KPMG had stolen information from the PCAOB as to what parts of KPMG's audits were under review by the PCAOB for being inadequate and insufficient. In addition, KPMG hired a former PCAOB examiner who still had access to PCAOB records. He helped KPMG establish a program in which KPMG employees could pass the ethics and integrity exam given by the PCAOB. After a lengthy negotiation in 2019, KPMG paid a $50 million fine and admitted that it had committed illegal actions.

The firms I examined didn't have $50 million in sales, much less the ability to pay such a fine. But it was still essential to make sure the audits were done correctly. And I had found an accounting firm that was looking a little shady.

Brownstein and Williams are a medium-sized Philadelphia firm with a little over $10 million in total sales. They were pretty well-known but certainly not one of the big boys. As I looked through some of their reports, it looked like they should have more audit deficiencies than were reported. I wasn't sure what it meant yet, but I could tell I would need to spend more time on them.

Just then, my phone rang. I answered, "Dr. Stone."

"Well, hello there, Dr. Stone. How is your day going?"

"I'm doing okay, Detective Levin, although I'm getting a bit tired of looking at spreadsheets and accounting ledgers."

Sharon chuckled, "Isn't that sort of what you do?"

"No, I'm a professor of accounting, so I teach other people how to do it. But this PCAOB work is getting a bit tedious. How is your day?"

"Just hanging around my desk today. There are no murders to investigate, just pushing all the paperwork onto someone else's desk. When are you going to head home?"

"Not sure. When are you finished?"

"I can pretty much leave any time. I put in my shift, and nothing is on my desk that can't wait until tomorrow. What do you want to do for dinner?"

I said, "I think it's time for some vegetarian Chinese food. Would that work for you?"

"Absolutely! Su Xing House over on Spruce is supposed to be really good. Want to try that?"

"Yep, and it's not far from my house. Why don't I meet you at the house in about thirty minutes, and we'll head over?"

Sharon replied, "Sounds great. Got any good ideas for dessert back at your place? I don't really care for the Chinese desserts."

"I've got some possibilities, but they would require that you disrobe to enjoy the entire experience truly."

Sharon laughed and said, "Whatever it takes to get a decent dessert!"

Ben and Sharon didn't know how much they needed to enjoy this night. Things were going to get very complicated for both of them very soon.

# Chapter Three

Rabinovich and Reznick gave two of their best enforcers, Mark Grinburg and Abram Moskowitz, the job of convincing Lev to sign the get. They told Grinburg and Moskowitz to use whatever means necessary to get the signature. They already had their $25 thousand retainer from Josef, but they wanted to get the balance.

Grinburg and Moskowitz knew where Lev's jewelry store was and that he closed at 7 pm. They waited until 6:45, seeing the last customers leaving the store. Once they were gone, Grinburg and Moskowitz entered the store.

Lev said, "Gentlemen, I hope you know what you want and can be quick about it. I close in 15 minutes."

Grinburg said, "You won't stay open a little extra to make a sale?"

"Normally I would, but I have an appointment tonight that I need to get to. Anyway, what can I get you?"

Moskowitz replied, "Actually, we are not here for jewelry. We are associates of your father-in-law, and we came here to encourage you to sign the get your wife wants."

"How the hell do you know about that?"

"As I mentioned, we are associates of Josef, and he asked us to help convince you that you should sign the get."

"First off, this is none of your business, whether you know my asshole father-in-law or not. Second, I have no intention of signing the get. My wife has embarrassed me by asking for one. She has shown no respect for our faith and traditions, and it will be a cold day before I give her what she wants."

While Grinburg came up behind Lev, Moskowitz said, "We were afraid that you might take that position." Grinburg put a handkerchief covered in chloroform over Lev's face. He was unconscious in a few seconds, and Grinburg caught him just as he was ready to fall.

The mobsters carried Lev to their car. They made it look like they were just talking to Lev in case anyone was watching. They opened the back door and shoved him on the seat.

Grinburg and Moskowitz had already planned for the possibility that Lev wouldn't easily cooperate. They knew of an abandoned factory not far from Red Lion Road. They had already gone there and broken the lock to get in easily.

They carried Lev into the warehouse, set him down on a chair, and tied his hands to the chair. Now it was just waiting until he came to, which took about 45 minutes.

As he slowly woke up, Lev said, "What the fuck is going on here? Why did you bring me here, and why am I tied to this chair?"

"Think of this as your chance to make it easy on yourself," said Grinburg. "All you have to do is sign this form, and we'll take you straight back to your store. Pretty easy to do, I think."

"I already told you I have no intention of signing that fucking form. My wife is going to stay my wife until I decide to divorce her."

Moskowitz smiled and said, "See, you've decided to do it the hard way. Actually, we were sort of hoping you would because we enjoy what's going to happen next." With that, he kicked Lev right in his balls.

Lev screamed and doubled over in the chair. He was panting, trying to get his breath. He could hardly raise his head.

Grinburg said, "So I think we have your attention now. As we said, we're not leaving without the signed get, so I would strongly encourage you just to sign the damn thing."

After he caught his breath, Lev said, "No! You can do whatever you like to me, but I'm not giving that bitch I married what she wants."

Moskowitz turned to Grinburg and said, "Tough guy, isn't he? I don't think he understands the lengths to which we will go." He kicked Lev in the balls one more time, but this time harder.

Lev doubled over again and could barely breathe. Grinburg leaned into Lev's face and said, "We can do this all night. We're in an abandoned factory, and there is no one close by who will hear you scream. Once again, I would strongly encourage you just to sign the form, and this can all be over."

Still trying to catch his breath, Lev shook his head no.

Grinburg said to Moskowitz, "Break out the taser. Mr. Hard Head here just doesn't seem to be able to make the right decision."

Moskowitz took the taser out of the backpack they carried with them. He took his time extracting the taser so that Lev had some time to watch him. When he finally had it out and turned on, he turned to Lev and said, "Last chance! Just sign the damn thing, and this all ends."

Again, Lev shook his head no. Moskowitz put the taser right on Lev's back and turned it on. Lev screamed, and the crackling of electricity ran through his body. Lev toppled over and looked like he had passed out. Grinburg took a cup of water and splashed it on Lev's face. Then he shook Lev until Lev seemed to come back to some level of consciousness.

Lev was still very groggy but seemed to have recovered from the shock enough to know where he was and the surroundings. Moskowitz leaned in this time and put his face right up to Lev's. "So that you know, my friend here and I actually enjoy doing this type of work. And we've got a full charge on the battery for this taser, so we can do this for a long time. In fact, the next time will be in a more delicate part of your anatomy."

Lev still sat there and shook his head no. Moskowitz said, "Okay, it's your nuts that you're getting roasted." With that, he put the taser on Lev's testicles and turned the switch.

Lev screamed at the top of his lungs, then toppled over again. Grinburg splashed his face with water again and tried to shake him awake. Lev didn't move.

Grinburg looked at Moskowitz and asked, "Do you think he's dead?"

Moskowitz put his fingers on Lev's neck. Nothing. Then he tried to get a pulse on Lev's wrist, and again nothing. "I think he's dead."

"Well, we tried to warn him. What do you think we should do?"

"Just leave the body here and get out. This place is so remote that no one will find him for a long time," replied Moskowitz.

"But does that mean that the bosses will still get paid? They will be pissed if they don't get the extra 25 large."

"I'm pretty sure that when the bosses tell that old guy what happened to his son-in-law, he'll pony up the money. Plus, with this dumb bastard dead, the wife will get the stupid-ass divorce she wants. Everyone is a winner except the guy strapped to the chair."

"Well, we did try to warn him, "smiled Grinburg.

# Chapter Four

Riva called her father early the following day to tell him that Lev had never come home the night before. Josef had already heard what had happened, other than where Lev's body was, and the Russian mobsters had told him it was time to pay up. But Josef knew he needed to make it look like he had no idea of Lev's whereabouts, so he told Riva that they would go out and look for Lev together.

The first thing they did was go check on Lev's store. They saw that the door was unlocked, but it didn't look like anything had been taken. Riva knew it was improbable that Lev had left the door open accidentally. Riva told her dad that she was going to call the police.

After only a few minutes, two officers, George Thomas and Fred Williams showed up at the store. They entered the store, and Riva was the one to greet them first. Everyone exchanged names.

Thomas said, "So what can we do for you?"

"My husband never made it home last night, leaving the door to his store open. He would never do either of those things," said Riva.

Both cops tried not to smile, but they both had been cops for a long time. They'd seen plenty of husbands and boyfriends just take off. They weren't going to jump to the conclusion that there was foul play involved.

Williams asked, "So you haven't seen him since he came to work yesterday?"

Riva replied, "No. I tried calling his cell phone several times, but it went to voice mail until I think the phone had just died. I was going to come over to the store, but I was afraid I might miss him at home. I stayed up almost all night, but I did drop off for a little while. Once I woke up, I called my dad, and we came over and saw the door to the store was unlocked. That's when we called you."

Thomas asked, "I'm assuming this behavior is unusual for your husband."

"Of course, it's unusual. My husband always comes straight home from work, and we have dinner with our kids."

"I can see on the door that the store normally closes at 7 pm," said Williams.

"Yes, except the store sometimes closes earlier on Friday, depending on when sunset occurs, and we start the Shabbat meal. But yesterday was a Wednesday, so he should have been home by 7:30, eight at the latest."

"Has your husband been acting differently or strangely lately?" inquired Thomas.

"My husband and I have been having some marital issues of late, but we are working through them," said Riva.

Both cops again tried not to smile. In their careers, they had heard too many times about marital problems, and suddenly someone was missing. It often means that one party or the other just decided to take off.

Riva said, "I can tell by the look in your eyes that you think my husband had had enough of me and just left. But we have three children whom we both adore, so there is no way he just left. Also, we are ultra-Orthodox Jews, and abandoning your family is just not done. Something happened to him."

Williams said, "We aren't jumping to conclusions. But there's not much we can do until he has been absent for 24 hours. That's the police policy regarding missing persons. But, in the meantime, do you have any ideas on where your husband would go other than home? Does he have family or friends in the area?"

Riva replied, "We have no family in the area other than my mother and father. Lev has relatives in New York but is not very close to them. But we are very close to our religious community.

We frequently have Shabbat meals at each other's home and attend shul at the same synagogue."

Thomas inquired, "Are there any particular names that would stand out? People he would go to first."

Riva replied, "No one who stands out. Lev spent most of his time at the store, with his family, and with our congregation. There are about 300 members in our shul, but no one who Lev was particularly close to."

Williams asked, "Mr. Goldstein, you haven't had much to say. Anything you can think of to add to trying to find your son-in-law."

Josef had plenty that he could have added, but then he would be heading off to jail. So, he just said, "Not really. My daughter covered all the important things. I can't really add anything. I liked my son-in-law and thought he was a good husband. I can't imagine what could have happened to him."

Thomas said, "Okay, here's what we can do. I'll leave both of you my card in case you hear anything. Once the 24 hours is up, I'll forward your case to the missing persons bureau. They're very good at tracking people down, so try to stay positive. I'm sure they'll be able to find your husband."

Both cops were thinking the exact same thing. Assuming he wants to be found.

# Chapter Five

The next afternoon Sharon was sitting in her office when the phone rang. She picked up the receiver and said, "Detective Levin."

"Sharon, it's Bill Simmons from Missing Persons. How are you doing?"

"Not bad, Bill. Mostly just catching up on paperwork right now. How are you doing?"

"Not bad, but I may have a case for you. You got any time right now?"

"Sure. The paperwork isn't leaving anytime soon. What's going on?"

"We got a missing person report late last night. This morning we started the case. The woman who filed the report couldn't tell us much, but she did say that her husband had a cell phone that had been on for a long time. We got the computer nerds to see if they could track back to where the phone was last on. Those folks may be nerdy, but they are damn good at what they do. They were able to pull the trail of the phone's whereabouts, and they found that the phone was last still on at an abandoned factory over on Red Lion. We just got over here and found the corpse of a guy who had really been worked over. CSI is on its way, but I thought I'd give you a call to see if you wanted to catch the case. Usually, I just go through the regular channels and let the hierarchy decide who gets a case, but this one is pretty weird, and I know you specialize in weird. I've heard about a female serial killer, vampires, and pirates."

"It's true I've caught some strange ones of late. Text me the address and I'll be right over."

Sharon called me, but I was in class, so she left a voicemail. "Hi there, Dr. Stone. You're probably busy educating the next generation, but I just wanted you to know that I may have caught a case. I don't know what it means for dinner tonight, but I'll be in touch."

Sharon got into her car and headed out. She had the Red Lion address only about 15 minutes from her office. As she pulled into the gate leading to the factory, she couldn't help but notice how run down the place was. But she thought to herself that someday, Toll Brothers or some other developer would put up a bunch of condos on the site.

She parked in front of what she thought was the entrance since a few vehicles were parked in front. She went in and immediately saw Simmons. "Bill, well, here I am."

Simmons came over to shake her hand and said, "Thanks for coming out so quickly. The CSI folks are just getting started. Come on over and take a look."

They made their way to where Lev was still strapped to the chair. CSI was still taking many pictures and had not yet unstrapped the body.

Sharon looked at the body and understood why Bill thought it was weird enough to call her. She could see where some electrical device had been used on the body's back and groin. Whoever it was had died an excruciating death.

She said to Simmons, "CSI got any idea what caused the burn marks?"

"They're thinking taser right now."

"So, a man was strapped to a chair and tasered on his shoulder and groin. Tortured! Who is this guy?"

"Lev Brodsky. He's an ultra-Orthodox Jew with a jewelry store in a shopping center a little way from here. His wife was the one who called in yesterday morning, but, as you know, we have to wait 24 hours before we can call it a missing person. We had a real break with the cell phone because no one would have thought to look out here. In fact, it doesn't even look like the guy was gagged. If he was screaming, and from the looks of this, he would have been, it's still too far away for anyone to hear it and call the cops."

Sharon went a little closer to the body. It was an ugly sight. She knew the taser on the shoulder would have hurt like hell, but a taser to the groin was brutal.

She asked Simmons, "ME been in for a cause of death yet?"

"No, he's been tied up with a hit-and-run murder in North Philly. But it sure looks like the taser to the balls took him out."

Sharon nodded and said, "Man, that is a nasty way to die. Electric shock must have just fried him. Heart attack, I would guess, but the ME will tell us for sure. Any idea who owns this place?"

"The City of Philadelphia. It was a tool manufacturing plant, but that business was sent overseas. The place was kept up for a while, but the owners finally decided to stop paying the taxes and let the place go to hell. Hasn't been used for anything in about a decade. And yeah, you probably think that some developer will eventually build McMansions or the like on this big a piece of ground, and they probably will, but it hasn't happened yet."

"Anybody tell the wife yet?"

"No, I was waiting for you. I'm not very good at reporting deaths. Usually, I'm just telling people that someone ran away or maybe overdosed in a cheap hotel. Don't see many cases as nasty as this one."

"So, you want me to do the death notification?"

"If you would. You've more experience with this type of notification than I do."

Sharon knew she really couldn't argue that much. "Okay, give me the address of the new widow, and I'll go over and break the news. And just so you know, it doesn't get any easier the more times you do it."

"I'm sure that is the case, and I appreciate your doing it. I admit my stomach got a little queasy when I first saw the body."

"Well, you're a guy, and taser to the balls had to rattle you a good bit. I'm a woman, and it made me a little sick."

Simmons gave Sharon the address of Lev's wife. She got back into her car and used Google Maps to find the directions to the location. Once she was on her way, she decided to call me.

I answered, "Dr. Stone."

"Hi, sweetness. Done with class for now?"

"I am. Got another one at 5 pm, but then I am free to find some delicious food."

"You didn't get my voicemail, did you?"

"Sorry, I've had a couple of students come by, and I didn't see it." What's going on?"

"I just caught a murder case over off of Red Lion. Old, abandoned factory. The guy strapped to a chair looks like he was tortured to death. Waiting on the ME for the final determination."

I said, "Tortured! Shit. Lady, you do get the best jobs, don't you?"

"That I do, but at least you're not involved in this one. Anyway, I have to go make a notification of death to the widow. She doesn't know anything yet other than her now-deceased husband was missing. She's the one who reported him gone. I've done a few of these notifications, and sometimes they're quick, and the family just starts crying. Still, sometimes you must spend time convincing the family that the police will do everything possible to find the murderer. My point is that I might be a little late tonight."

I said, "Not a problem. We can get Mexican takeout or something. I would guess that you need a drink more than food. Maybe two."

"After looking at the body, I'm not sure two will do it. I'll tell you more when I get home."

"Sounds like I should open up a nice red Merlot and start to let it breathe."

"That and make sure there is some vodka in the freezer. This one is really revolting."

# Chapter Six

Josef knew that he had to get the money to the Russians, but he also knew he had to make it look like he was concerned about Lev. He said to his daughter, "Don't worry, Riva. I'm sure that Lev is okay. Maybe he just decided to go to New York to see his family. He hasn't seen them in a while."

"Dad, you know that's not true! There is no way that he would willingly just leave with no phone call or anything. We may have some marital problems, but he cares about his children. He would never do anything to make them worry. Something bad has happened; I just know it."

"No, Riva. Let's don't jump to conclusions. The police may find him at any time." He felt guilty about lying directly to his daughter, but he knew he couldn't tell her what he knew. If fact, he couldn't tell anyone.

At just that moment, Riva's cell phone buzzed. She pressed the button and said, "Hello."

"Hello. Is this Ms. Riva Brodsky?"

"Yes, who is this?"

"I'm Detective Sharon Levin. I was wondering if it would be okay if I came to your home to speak for a few minutes?"

Riva screamed. She turned and yelled at her father, "I told you something was really wrong. It's the police."

Josef took Riva's cell and said to Sharon, "Hello, I am Riva's father, Josef. What do you need to talk to her about?"

"It's about your son-in-law, Lev. I'm afraid I have some bad news, but I would like to tell Ms. Brodsky in person."

"My daughter is screaming and crying because she's afraid for Lev. Can you tell me what happened, and I will pass along the information?" Josef figured the less he was around the police now, the better.

"Actually, that's not our policy. I'll only take a few minutes of your time if you allow me to come over."

Josef relented and said, "Fine, but understand that my daughter is upset already."

"I will be as quick as I can be, and I'll try to be as kind and understanding as possible."

Josef turned to Riva and said, "A Detective Levin is on her way over. She said that she only needed a few minutes."

Riva was still crying but had calmed down some. She told her dad, "I told you something horrible had happened!"

Sharon arrived at Riva's house in ten minutes. She knocked on the door, and Josef came to the door. He said, "Detective Levin, I assume."

"I am."

"Please come in. My daughter is in the living room."

Sharon went into the living room and introduced herself to Riva. Riva shook her hand very softly. Sharon said, "Ms. Brodsky, I am very sorry that I have bad news. Your husband, Lev, was found dead over at an abandoned factory on Red Lion. I am very sorry for your loss."

Riva dropped her head down and started to sob. She slowly got together and asked, "Do you have any idea what happened?"

"We are still gathering evidence right now, so I can't tell you that much right now. But I want to assure you that my colleagues and I are going to do everything possible to find out what happened to your husband."

Josef asked, "Where is his body right now?"

"He is being examined by the Crime Scene Unit and the Medical Examiner right now, but we should have it wrapped up in a few hours. Just so you know, I am Jewish, so I know it is important to have the body buried very quickly. We will make every effort to make sure you can follow your religious rituals properly and on time."

Riva nodded her head. Josef asked, "Since you understand our religious rites, you know that my family needs to begin sitting shiva very quickly. And Lev's children have not been told anything yet, so we need to have that challenging discussion. But we need to do it quickly, so could you please leave? We appreciate your coming in person to tell us, but my daughter and the rest of our family need to be together right now to begin the mourning process."

"I certainly understand. The body will need to be held for a few hours down at the morgue. I will have someone from that department contact you as soon as the body can be released to you. Again, I am very sorry for your loss, and I want to assure you that we will do everything we can to find out what happened to your husband."

Sharon left the house, and Josef bent over his daughter. He put his arm around Riva and said, "Don't worry, Riva. I'm sure the police will find out what happened to Lev, and we will do everything we can to help them."

Of course, naturally, he had absolutely no intention of helping, and he prayed that the police would find nothing. He knew that if the police found anything involving the Russian Mob, it would eventually get back to him. He just needed to pay these murderers and hope that they left him alone.

Josef knew he would have to say Kaddish at Lev's funeral and would be expected to have some kind, comforting words to say about his son-in-law. As much as he hated Lev, he didn't mean for him to die. He just wanted him to sign the get.

Why couldn't he just sign the damn thing?

# Chapter Seven

I was sitting at home, thumbing through some more of the documents that the PCAOB had sent me, waiting for Sharon to get home. One thing that struck me was that the accounting firm of Brownstein and Williams was looking more and more like they had not been handling their audits appropriately. Their audits were particularly sparse for one of their clients named Petrovsky Markets. Petrovsky Markets had some outstanding loans that required that they be audited each year. In addition, they had to provide their tax returns to their bank: First American Bank.

Petrovsky Markets included three medium-sized grocery stores up in Northeast Philly. They catered predominately to the Russian crowd, with many Russian food and beverages available. Not surprisingly, pierogis were very popular with many choices. The stores carried a lot of red caviar, which is much cheaper than the black type. They had a large selection of the famous Russian breads, and they all carried the unique honey that is only available from the Altai mountains. Actually, reading about all this food was getting me hungry. I was starting to hope that Sharon would get home soon.

What struck me as unusual was that it didn't seem that the three stores weren't doing very well financially. The three stores barely broke even according to their financial statements and tax returns. Yet all three stores had been in business for many years, and their bank didn't seem worried about how they were doing. The three markets were small enough that Brownstein and Williams did some traditional auditing by hand, not just internal control examinations, as is done with bigger firms. Yet their cash flow statements didn't seem consistent with how much was coming in and how much was being spent on the products the markets sold. I knew that many smaller companies use cash a lot, and some of it doesn't make it on the books. Restaurants often have very few "employees" as everyone is paid under the table. But it was somewhat strange for a market to do it. Again, their cash flow statements showed that they had a good amount of cash coming through their system. Still, the amounts were significantly beyond what their tax returns and financial statements would seem to indicate they should have.

I knew that one of the keys to money laundering is getting cash from illegal operations into the traditional banking system. Once the money has been "cleaned" into the system, it can be sent anywhere and is very hard to track. I wasn't sure yet that there were unsavory activities going on with this company, but what I had seen already convinced me that I would have to do some more digging.

My cellphone buzzed, and I saw it was Sharon. I said, "Hello, beautiful. Are you coming home soon?"

"I'll be on my way to your place soon. But first, I must stop at my place to shower and change clothes."

"It was that bad a day?"

"Bad enough that I need a restart. I need to wash some of the stink off me, figuratively speaking. I had to do a death notification, which was really tough."

I replied, "I'm sure it was. Take your time. Call me when you've left your house, and I'll put in an order for Mexican if that's still good for you."

"That's fine. Just make sure there is alcohol of some sort also available. Could be wine, beer, or liquor, but something."

"I'll make sure to have all three choices available." We hung up.

Sharon must have had an awful day. It's not like she's a teetotaler, but she doesn't usually drink that much, and she rarely seemed to need a drink as she does now. I had wine and vodka, and I could pick up some Coronas at the Mexican restaurant when I picked up the food. If she needed to get hammered, I could undoubtedly oblige!

I knew I still had a little time before I needed to order the food, so I went back to Petrovsky Markets and their financial statements. Their financial statements showed what appeared to be a minimal number of employees, even for an under-the-table type of company. This seemed very unlikely to me as I knew it takes several employees to keep the store shelves stocked, respond to customer needs, and then get them checked out. I did enough audits in my public accounting days to know how many employees it takes per $100,000 sales. The number of Petrovsky's employees looked too low compared to their sales.

So, they pay some employees under the table! Not really a big deal as a lot of smaller companies do that. It's certainly a version of tax evasion, but even CPAs don't get too excited about it. We would warn the client that they were breaking tax law, but we didn't go into their books and try the tease out who was being paid under the table. Most CPA firms feel that they are doing their duty by notifying their clients, in writing, that they are engaging in tax fraud. Up to them to do something about it. But if paying their employees off the books means money laundering is going on, the auditors had to examine that in detail. It looked like Brownstein and Williams were doing some of that.

Then something popped up that caught my eye. I saw that Petrovsky's fees to Brownstein and Williams looked very high compared to what I knew to be the normal range. CPA firms vary a good deal in what they charge for an audit engagement, but there is usually a ceiling that they all adhere to. Brownstein's fees looked at least twice the norm for a client the size of Petrovsky Markets. I made a note that I needed to look into this further.

My cellphone buzzed, and I saw it was Sharon. "Hi. Ready for some Mexican food?"

"You bet, but make sure there are plenty of libations at the ready. This was a rough, rough day."

"Want some Coronas to wash down the Mexican?"

"That's good for dinner, but I think I'll need a vodka martini, shaken, not stirred, as an appetizer."

"I'm sure James Bond would approve. I'll call in our usual Mexican order, include some Coronas, and have the martini shaker ready when you get here."

"You definitely have my best interests at heart. Maybe we'll come up with something more entertaining to have for dessert."

"Don't tease me!"

# Chapter Eight

A meeting had been set up for Josef to hand over the additional $25K to the Russian Mob. They were to meet at a Russian restaurant off Roosevelt Boulevard at noon. Josef had the money, in hundreds, in an envelope. He only wanted to hand over the cash and return to set up for the funeral he had helped cause.

He pulled into the parking lot of the restaurant and locked his car. He entered the door to the restaurant and began looking for the people he was to meet. The waiter came over and asked if he was Josef Goldstein, and he replied yes. The waiter said that some people were waiting to see him in the back of the store. Leaving the comfy confines of having witnesses made him a bit nervous, but he entered the back of the store anyway.

Once, he was in a server in the back, pointed at a small room off to the side. Josef went in and saw two guys he didn't know: Grinburg and Moskowitz. Grinburg motioned for him to sit down.

Grinburg said, "So, Mr. Goldstein, I assume you are satisfied with our work and have our money."

Josef replied, "Yes, I have your money." He took out the envelope. "But I have to ask: Why did you have to kill him? That wasn't part of the deal. I just wanted you to get him to sign the get."

"Your now late son-in-law was not cooperating," said Grinburg. "We tried very hard to get him to sign the damned thing, but he was being difficult, and as we continued to encourage him, things got out of hand. Shit happens. What can I say?"

Josef nodded slowly and said, "Are you sure no one will find out what happened? I've already had a police detective come to my daughter's home to tell her about the death. I'm sure the police will do some investigating, and I want to make sure nothing comes out about our arrangement."

Moskowitz said, "Don't worry. We were cautious. We are very good at our jobs, so even if the police investigate, they're not going to find anything."

Again, Josef nodded and handed the envelope to Grinburg. "Here is the balance of what I owe you. I have to say that I hope we never meet again."

Grinburg and Moskowitz smiled, and Grinburg said, "Well, that's not exactly how things will go. Our bosses want you to spread the word in the ultra-Orthodox community that if anyone else needs some help obtaining a get, we are here to help. Oh, and the price went up an additional $25 grand for the accommodation we just delivered."

Josef choked a bit and said softly, "What do you mean the price went up? We had a deal."

Grinburg smiled again and said, "Yeah, but our bosses feel that since your son-in-law was killed, the price needs to reflect the additional services provided."

Josef tried to keep his composure and said, "But I didn't want you to kill him. That was not part of the plan. Why should I pay extra for something that I didn't want?"

Moskowitz grinned and replied, "Josef, you don't seem to understand. This is not a request. This is a demand. The price has gone up, and you're going to pay it. We are not negotiating here. We'll give you a little time to gather the funds, but we expect payment within three days."

"But I don't have that kind of money. I was barely able to get the $50,000 together. I don't have $25,000 that I can just hand over to you. I'm not a rich man."

"What your finances are like is not our problem," said Grinburg. "We just expect payment in three days. And before you even ask what happens if you don't pay, let's just say that you don't want to go down that road. It's not a pleasant highway to travel."

Josef choked some more and replied, "But I told you. I don't have another $25,000, and I have no way to get it. Also, I can't spread the word at my shul that you are helping women get a divorce decree. Everyone in the shul would put together that I was behind what happened to Lev. They would inform the police, and I would be arrested."

"And I will remind you," said Grinburg, "that those issues are your problem, not ours. We expect to see the 25 large in three days, and we may ask ourselves to see if you've spread the word about our new service. As I said, you don't want to get on our wrong side. Just do what we say, and you'll be fine."

Josef looked down at the floor and thought: This whole thing has been anything but fine, and it probably wasn't ever going to be okay. He didn't know what he would do, but he didn't like any of his options.

Why couldn't his dumb-ass son-in-law just sign the damned thing?

# Chapter Nine

Sharon usually gets up much earlier than I do. She's a homicide cop, and there's always something that needs to be investigated. I'm an accounting professor, and some grading can always wait. There have to be some perks associated with my job.

Sharon got to her office at 7:30 am. She knew that she needed to get cracking on the murder at the factory. She saw that the Medical Examiner had already filed his preliminary report on her desk.

The report didn't actually add anything to what she already knew. The victim had been tortured with an electrical device. The ME believed it was likely a taser, but he admitted that it could have been another type of electrical apparatus. The ME report indicated that the victim had been tied to the chair for some time because of the bruises and cuts on his arms. The electrical device would have caused the victim to lurch and pull against the restraints, but the ME believed some damage was done before the electricity kicked in. He had not begun the autopsy yet but felt the cause of death was a heart attack brought on by the electrical shock. He noted that the victim was relatively young, and it was somewhat surprising that the electric shock would be deadly. The ME suggested that he will have to look for evidence of heart disease or the like when he does the autopsy.

Just then, Sharon's phone rang. "Detective Levin."

"Sharon, it's Mike Durham from the ME's office. We've got a problem."

"It's a little early to have problems already, but Mike, go ahead and hit me with it."

"The guy's family killed at the factory will not allow me to perform an autopsy. They say that the guy must be buried today, and I can't get the autopsy done that quickly."

"But, Mike, we've had autopsies performed on Jewish murder victims. We had one just last year, as a matter of fact. And, as you know, I'm Jewish and know that autopsies are allowed according to Jewish law. There needs to be a good reason for the autopsy, you can't just do one, but I would say that finding more evidence about the torture and killing of one of their own would qualify as a good reason."

Durham replied, "That's what I tried to tell the widow's father, but he is obstinate and said he doesn't want his son-in-law's body defiled by having an autopsy done. He wants to have the funeral later today, and there is no way I can get it done by then."

"Doesn't the victim have some family here? Don't they get a vote?"

"Apparently, the victim has some cousins in New York who are coming down, but the father-in-law is saying that his daughter doesn't want the autopsy done and that her vote counts the most. He is already trying to have the body removed from the morgue."

Sharon shook her head a bit and said, "I have the number for the father-in-law and the wife, but I doubt they will pick up the phone because they are likely already sitting shiva. I'm going to have to take a ride over there. I'm not even sure they'll let me in the house, but I will give it a try."

"Thanks for the help. This is a little out of my area, so anything you can do to convince them that an autopsy will assist in finding the murderer would be helpful. You know my number, so call me when you have anything."

While Sharon was driving over to Riva's home, Josef was busy trying to ensure that there was no autopsy done on Lev. Josef did have religious reasons that Lev should be buried soon, but mostly Josef didn't want the Medical Examiner's office to look too closely into Lev's death. Josef knew almost nothing about how an autopsy is done, but the less time the authorities had to look at Lev's body, the less time they had to find something that might implicate Josef.

He felt somewhat guilty about not following Jewish traditions, but he'd already broken a big one by getting Lev killed. He had not meant to get him killed, but that didn't change the fact that Josef set the whole thing in motion. He would have a lot to atone for at the next Yom Kippur!

Josef had called on members of his shul to gather and form a minyan of the required ten men to say Kaddish. He knew all the men quite well, and all were very sorry for the death of Lev and more than happy to be part of the minyan. Josef thought he was excelling at pretending to be mourning his son-in-law's death, but it wasn't easy. He knew someone might wonder why if he didn't show the proper remorse. He couldn't take that chance, so he looked as sad as possible.

While all the mourning was going on, Josef was also trying to figure out how to raise the additional $25K that the mobsters demanded. He didn't have it in his bank account or in his home. And because of sitting shiva, he wasn't allowed to leave his daughter's home, so it would be complicated to get the money even if he figured out a way to do it. And he also was becoming worried that the mobsters would just continue to demand more money. Where would it end? But all he could focus on right now was getting them the $25,000, and maybe they would leave him alone.

As Josef sat on the couch, there was a knock at the door. He decided to answer it because it might be the ME with news about retrieving Lev's body.

He opened the door and saw that it was the detective. He said, "I hope you have information about releasing my son-in-law's body. My family is distraught that we can't properly bury Lev at a proper time."

Sharon replied, "That's what I'm here to discuss. I know you are sitting shiva, but may I come in?"

"There is nothing to discuss. I know you are aware of our traditions, so the only question is when Lev's body will be released."

Since it was clear that she wouldn't be invited in, Sharon decided to talk outside. She and Josef stepped away from the front door. "Mr. Goldstein, I know about the rituals, but I also know that your son-in-law was murdered. We need a little more time for the ME to examine the body to see if we can gather any additional information that might assist us in finding the murderer. I'm sure you want the murderer found, so if you could just give us one more day, we might discover something important."

Josef didn't want to give them extra time, but he also knew that he needed to at least pretend to be concerned about finding the murderer. He had tried to play the card that Lev's got to be buried that day, but this detective seemed relentless. He thought for a minute and said, "Of course, we want to find the murderer! Someone killed my son-in-law, and I want that person found and prosecuted. But our traditions are central to our lives, and we want them preserved."

"Mr. Goldstein, we will do everything possible to uncover this horrendous act's culprits, but we need your help. One extra day is all we are asking for. Could you please ask your daughter if that would be acceptable to her?"

Josef knew that if he hindered the investigation, that could look very bad, maybe even suspicious. Plus, how much could they gather from just one day? "Fine, I will ask Riva for her blessing to postpone for one day."

Josef went into the house and sat next to his daughter. He said to her, "Riva, the police detective is out front. She says the Medical Examiner needs one more day to complete the autopsy. Doing it will maybe help find the scum who killed Lev. Is it okay with you to wait one day before he is released from the morgue?"

Riva replied, "If it helps them find out how killed Lev, I am fine with waiting the extra time. In fact, if it takes more than one day, that's okay, too."

Josef knew he didn't want to offer any extra time, but he also knew it might look strange, maybe even incriminating, if he didn't provide the extra day. He returned to the porch and said to Sharon, "My daughter has agreed to allow one extra day. We expect to have the body released tomorrow afternoon without any hassles from anyone."

"I thank you for giving us the additional time. I can't promise it will make a difference, but it might. We will be in touch by noon tomorrow." With that, Sharon left the porch and headed for her car.

Josef stood for a moment and thought he couldn't decide if he wanted them to find anything. The more they uncovered about Lev's death, the more likely they would somehow link him to the murder.

It was a very tight rope that he was walking.

# Chapter Ten

Sharon warned me that night she would be swamped for the next few days. She gave me a brief rundown of how the victim's family only gave the ME one extra day to do the autopsy because of Jewish traditions. Sharon said that she understood their need for the burial to happen quickly, but she did mention that the father-in-law didn't seem as concerned about finding the murderer or murderers as she would have thought he should be. She said she didn't know what it meant, if anything, but she would keep it in the back of her mind. Seemed just a little weird.

Even though I didn't have a class today, I decided to come into my office and do some PCAOB work. Lately, I've found that I'm not being that productive at home. I seem to go through phases of having focus at home and little at the office, and sometimes I need to go in because there are too many distractions at home. Today was a go-in day.

Usually, I don't have office hours or meetings on days I don't teach, so I just went straight to my office and closed the door. I already had my coffee, so I could hopefully keep a low profile and get some work done. It's not that I dislike my colleagues, but when I'm on a deadline, as I am with my current PCOAB assignments, I try not to spend too much time chatting around the office.

I fired up my laptop and opened my PCAOB files. I found myself drawn directly to the Brownstein and Williams' file. I couldn't seem to figure out what was bugging me, but something was. I looked at the PCAOB analysis of how Brownstein and Williams had conducted their audit of the Petrovsky markets.

As I noted in my previous analysis of Petrovsky markets, it looked like the three markets were getting by, but their cash flow statements showed the markets doing very well. I had seen enough financial fraud cases to suspect some money was hidden in the markets. But I just couldn't figure out how it was being done.

Then I had a lightbulb come on: the Financial Crimes Enforcement Network (FinCEN). FinCEN was established in 1990 as an agency whose primary objective was to combat money laundering and terrorist funding. Post 9/11, the Patriot Act expanded FinCEN's authority and made it an official bureau of the Department of Treasury.

I knew I couldn't just call FinCEN and expect to get any attention. My case was minuscule compared to what FinCEN typically sees. But I did have a friend in high places, Emily Keen from the FBI. We had worked together on the Outer Banks case. I thought that she might have some contacts who might be able to get me some financial info about Petrovsky.

I just decided to take a chance and called Emily's number. She picked up after two rings. "Keen."

"Emily, it's Ben Stone from down at the Outer Banks."

"Ben, it's great to hear from you. Just the other day, I was thinking about all the fun we had down in North Carolina and that we were still able to find time to capture some Jamaican mobsters."

"It was quite an exciting few days. Anyway, I'm working on a case for the PCAOB, and I need a little financial info that I can't access. Any chance you know someone at the Financial Crimes Enforcement Network?"

"FinCEN! Yeah, I do have a woman I've done some work with before, Mikayla Heston. She's a good person and a world-class financial researcher. Why? You want me to get you an introduction?"

"Maybe, but I have to ask if you think she would be insulted if I asked her about a little company here in Philly that has three Russian markets. FinCEN generally focuses on billions of dollars, not a few million. I'm sure my little case would never hit their radar, but I thought maybe she could find the answers I need pretty quickly."

"Believe it or not, Mikayla is very down-to-earth, which is unusual for anyone working with the Treasury. I haven't talked to her in a while, but I'm happy to give her a buzz to see what her workload is like. Give me a brief rundown of what you're looking at."

I replied, "I'm looking at a medium-sized accounting firm in the area. Some of their audit work looks shabby, and I've focused on one client, Petrovsky Markets. They have three stores and gross about $10 million a year. I know that's rounding error to FinCEN, but it's important to my work. I just need someone who could quickly pull some info about the company's cash transactions. Basically, I need a little help getting data from their bank, a place called First American Bank."

"Doesn't sound like the thing that would take Mikayla a lot of time. Let me call her, and one of us will get back to you."

"Thanks so much!"

While waiting for Emily or Mikayla to call back, I continued to delve into the financial records at Petrovsky a little more. While my information wasn't conclusive, it sure looked a little fishy. A lot of cash was moving around, and it was unclear how that cash had been generated. Petrovsky wasn't involved with any casinos, which is a prime source of money laundering, so that wasn't it. Drug money has to be laundered, so maybe that was one of the ways cash found its way onto the Petrovsky books. But that seemed unlikely, too, because big bundles of $100 bills must be moved into the banking system. Not easy to with a couple of markets in NE Philly.

My phone rang, and I answered, "Ben Stone."

"Ben, my name is Mikayla Heston of FinCEN. Emily Keen of the FBI gave me your number and said you had a small case you're working on in which I may be able to help."

"Mikayla, thanks so much for calling me. Emily may have already told you that I'm an accounting professor at Temple University, but I also am doing some consulting for the Public Company Accounting Oversight Board. They investigate if accounting firms follow proper audit procedures if you're unfamiliar with them. I've got a medium-sized firm here in Philadelphia that I'm examining and one of their clients looks a little shady."

"Emily gave me a quick rundown. I'm guessing you would like me to pull some of the bank statements for the perhaps shady client?"

"I like someone who cuts to the chase. Yes, that is exactly what I'm looking for. I'm just trying to see if the cash they're showing on their financial statements matches up to their bank statements. But this is a small company and a minor issue by your standards. You sure you have time to do this?"

Mikayla replied, "Ben, it shouldn't take me that long. I'm sure you know that we chase drug cartels, terrorists, and billions of dollars. We have some sophisticated software we use to look for the money trail to do that type of work. Why don't you email me a list of the company names, employer ID numbers, and anything else you think might help you? My email address is mheston@fincen.gov. I've got a little work I need to do right now, but I can probably run those companies through our databases later today and see what pops up.

"Mikayla, that would be fantastic! I appreciate your assistance."

"No problem. I'll be in touch when I find something."

I hung up and immediately called Emily. "Emily, it's Ben. I just got off the phone with Mikayla Heston, and she's willing to do a little digging for me. Thank you so much for putting me in touch with her."

"No worries, Ben. We lovers of the Outer Banks have to stick together. I hope Mikayla can get you some info to assist your efforts."

"Me, too. If you find yourself up here in Philly, please let me know. Sharon and I know some great places if you like blues and jazz. We would be pleased to treat you to some music and good Cajun-style food."

"I'll keep it in mind. Good luck."

For the first time since I started this examination, I finally felt like I was making some progress. Of course, being an accountant, I knew from experience that feeling like and actually making progress were two very different things!

# Chapter Eleven

Sharon got a call from the ME at about 10 am. He said that he had something he wanted to show her about the autopsy. She jumped into her car and headed over to the ME's office.

When she got to the office, she went straight into the lab. Dr. Durham was waiting for her in the autopsy room. "So, Mike, you said you have something to tell me."

"I do, but it's not exactly from me. It's mostly from the CSI group. While doing the autopsy, I found some hair follicles that didn't look the same as the victim. I gathered them and forwarded them to the CSI lab with specimens from the victim. They quickly analyzed the DNA and found that the hair follicles didn't match the victim. Then they did an additional rapid test on the DNA and found that the hair was from someone who is an Ashkenazi Jew."

"You got all that in less than a day?"

"I knew that you were under the gun to get the body released, so we expedited everything. I'm not sure if the DNA info will lead you to the killer, but it's maybe something."

Sharon replied, "I'm not sure how much it will help either. I know that there are almost 200,000 Jewish households in Philly, so that is a lot of ground to cover. It does narrow the search a lot, but it still doesn't home in on a possible culprit. Also, we thought this whole thing might be Jewish-related since the victim was an ultra-Orthodox Jew. The ultra-Orthodox Jewry pretty much stays to themselves."

"I know. But it does mean that you can narrow your investigation some. I'm sure you would focus on the victim's known acquittances, but if you get a lead on a suspect, and if you can get a DNA sample, you now have something to compare it to. Anyway, I thought it was a start."

"It is a start, and I appreciate it. Anything else that you've found that I should know about?"

Durham responded, "Not that much, but judging by the burns on this guy's clothes and even his back and groin, whoever did this held the electric device, probably a taser, on his body for a decent amount of time. Whoever did this wasn't playing around. They tortured this guy. In fact, I would guess that the groin shock was held on his body for a few seconds. Not just a buzz. This guy went through a lot. Whatever the murderers wanted him to do or not do must have been pretty damned important to them. I know that I would have told them whatever they wanted in a hurry. Not that I'm a wus, but it would be pretty damn important for me to subject myself to that type of abuse."

"I hear you. Anyway, when do you think you can release the body?"

"I can probably be done around 4 pm. Do you think the victim's family will be satisfied?"

"I guess they're going to have to be. By the way, I've got to tell you something. While the victim's wife was very supportive of uncovering any clues, her father seemed in a hurry to get this investigation over. I understand getting the body released, but the guy doesn't seem interested in finding out who killed his son-in-law. It's a little weird."

"Funny you mention that. I've done autopsies for Jews before, and I've never been pushed as hard as this family is pushing to get the body released. Most seem more interested in trying to find justice than adhering to Jewish law. Did the father-in-law like his son-in-law?"

"I'm not sure, but I think I may have to look into that some. Anyway, thanks for expediting everything. I've got to head back to the office to do some investigating before the trail gets cold."

Durham replied, "Happy to help. I'll let you know when the body is released. Keep me in the loop as far as the investigation goes. I'm a little more interested in this one than I usually am. Most of the time, I just do my job, but this one is creepy enough to warrant a little extra.

"Not a problem. I'll be in touch if we make any progress."

While Sharon and Durham were discussing the case, Josef was busy trying to figure out a way to get the Mob their money. He had some savings, but his wife kept track of their money, and she would undoubtedly notice $25,000 missing if they even had that much. So that avenue was out.

Then he hit upon a possibility: The jewels in Lev's store. He knew that Lev locked up his most expensive gems in a safe, but he probably didn't have time to put them away before the mobsters took him. In fact, the jewels were perhaps still in the storefront.

Josef knew the store had been locked and probably had the yellow crime scene tape everywhere, but he knew that Riva had an emergency key to the store and where she hid it. Maybe he could appease the mobsters if he got the key and could secure some jewels. He knew he didn't have the time and resources to convert the gems to cash, but if he gave the mobsters enough jewelry, they might be satisfied. It was a bit chancy, but he had few choices.

The immediate problem was that he was not supposed to leave Riva's home while they were sitting shiva. The only appropriate reasons to leave the home were going to the synagogue or Shabbat. He couldn't just say he was running out to the store. He decided the only thing to do was tell another lie and say to Riva that their rabbi wanted him to come to the shul to discuss the funeral arrangements. He felt very guilty about it, but he was stuck. Lying to his daughter was wrong, but getting roughed up, maybe killed, by the mobsters was very scary, and telling another lie was likely his only way to avoid that.

This year, he would have much to atone for during the High Holidays!

# Chapter Twelve

I was still plowing through the info I had from Brownstein and Williams when I got a call.

"Ben Stone."

"Hi, Ben. It's Mikayla Heston from FinCEN. I think I have some of the information you're looking for."

"Wow, that was quick! You folks sure move fast."

"As I said, we already have algorithms to do some of the analysis we need. And one of the first things we look for is how much cash a company or even a person is getting into the financial system. As you know, I'm sure; once the cash gets into the financial system, the money can be moved worldwide. So, we have to move fast, thus the algorithms."

"So, does it look like my little Russian markets are engaging in unsavory activities?"

Mikayla replied, "I pulled up all their cash transactions for the past three years with First National Bank. Based on what you sent me about their financial statements, the numbers do not add up. More cash is funneling through the bank than the company shows on its books. But that's not the big thing."

"Let me guess. A lot of deposits are going in just under the $10,000 threshold for bank reporting."

"That's exactly it. In one year alone, they had 157 deposits that were just over $9,000 each but under the 10K reporting requirement. Ben, that's a very telltale sign that something fishy is going on with these markets."

"157 deposits! That's almost a million and a half dollars right there. For a business that typically grosses about ten mill a year."

Mikayla said, "I'm sure they do a lot of cash business. Small stores have many customers who don't use debit or credit cards, and even fewer still use checks. But it's the $10,000 threshold that's the red flag. What is really disturbing is that the bank could certainly see this activity. According to the records I found, the bank has never reported any suspicious activity to the IRS. Our databases crosscheck with the IRS databases, and again I see no reports at all to the IRS."

"So, it's pretty clear something fishy is going on, but we're just not sure what. And I'm not sure what this says about the accounting firm yet. The Russian markets are small enough that Brownstein and Williams would likely do a traditional audit, not just an internal control. Doing an old-style audit would mean they would be looking at the cash balance at the end of the year, not the daily or weekly cash transactions. But Brownstein and Williams is required by the PCAOB to engage in some appropriate internal control procedures even if they're not using them directly for their audit."

"I'm not an accountant," said Mikayla, "But that makes sense to me. Anyway, I have the reports that I will email to you. Maybe you will find them helpful."

"Mikayla, they've already proved helpful. And thank you so much for getting them for me. I really appreciate it a lot."

"No problem. Let me know if anything else comes up that I can help with. And please give Emily my best."

"I will certainly do so."

With that, I hung up. I couldn't say I'd solved the issues, but I was progressing. I just wasn't sure where it was going to take me. It was clear already that I would have a negative report for the PCAOB on Brownstein and Williams, but it seemed there might be more to it than just lax auditing. It wasn't really my responsibility to dig deeper than finding lousy auditing. Still, being with Sharon for so long, when I see potential illegal activity going on, I can't help myself. I had to do a little more digging.

While I was continuing my analysis of Brownstein and Williams and Petrovsky Markets, Josef contacted the Russian Mob to give them the balance of what they said he owed. He had found

Riva's key to Lev's store, told her that their rabbi wanted to see him about funeral arrangements to justify leaving Riva's home, and had gotten into the store to gather what he believed was over $25,000 in jewelry. Josef had worked some in Lev's store, so he had an idea of the jewelry's worth, and he added what he believed to be over $5,000 extra to satisfy the mobsters that he had done what they asked. They had left Josef a phone number and set up a meeting at a small café not far from Bustleton Avenue.

When Josef arrived, he was surprised that the henchmen didn't show. Rabinovich, Reznick, and a guy named Kaplan, the head guys, were all seated at a table in the back. Josef slowly made his way to the table and had a seat.

Rabinovich said, "So Josef, I assume you have the additional 25 large we require."

Josef replied, "As I told your other men, I don't have $25,000 at my disposal. But I have brought you at least $25,000 in gold and jewelry. It's in this pouch." He handed the bag over to Rabinovich.

Rabinovich opened the bag and took a peek. There was what appeared to be a fair amount of gold and jewelry. But Rabinovich closed the bag and said, "Two things. First, we deal in cash. Second, how do we know this jewelry isn't fake?"

"I told your man there was no way I could come up with $25,000 in cash. That's why I added some extra to what I gave you. And do I look stupid enough to try to con you guys? It would be unwise of me to try to pull one over on you. It's real gold and jewelry."

Reznick chimed in and said, "He's right. He's not dumb enough to try to con us. I'm sure he knows that would be a horrible idea!" With that, Reznick patted Josef on the arm.

Rabinovich grinned and said, "That's probably true. Okay, we'll take the jewels and see what we can get for them. We know how to get in touch if you come up short, and we'll be back. However, we do have a couple of other things to discuss."

Josef shivered and said, "What else could there be?"

Rabinovich kept his grin and said, "First, we want to know if you've spread the word through your people about our willingness to help with similar types of needs. Any woman who needs a get, we can be of assistance."

"I'm supposed to be sitting shiva for my son-in-law. I can't be suggesting what you say right now. In fact, I'm not sure I can do it at all because won't it look suspicious? Lev is dead, and now I'm telling people I know someone who can help with a get. Am I not putting all of us at risk?"

Kaplan decided to jump in and said, "It means you need to be very discreet. We're not asking you to put up a sign on the wall. Keep your ears open and if something sounds promising, let us know. We'll take it from there."

Josef still had no idea how to pull this off, but he nodded. He then said, "And what else do we need to discuss?"

Kaplan leaned in and whispered, "Don't get any bright ideas about going to the police."

"Why would I even think of doing that? I didn't kill Lev, but I was involved so that I would get in trouble."

Kaplan replied, "If the cops start to uncover what really happened, they might look to cut you a good deal if you turn us in. Don't even think about it. We have many associates in the area, and if any or all of us are arrested, things will go badly for your daughter and the rest of your family. In short, don't do something stupid. It would be very bad."

It seemed that Josef was shivering through this meeting, but now he was shaking. When he first went to these mobsters, he thought they would just scare Lev, and Riva would get the get. Now he's sitting in a café having doled out $50,000 in cash, handed over a bunch of jewelry, and being threatened if he says anything.

All he could think of to do was nod. And he kept asking to himself: Why couldn't Lev just have signed the thing?

# Chapter Thirteen

Sharon and I both had had pretty tough days. She had been under the gun to get as much info as possible from the ME before the body. I felt I had made decent progress on my PCAOB work, but I knew I had more to do. I thought we should just take the night off, get some Chinese takeout, kick back, and relax. But I also knew we would have to debrief some because that's how we are.

While waiting for Sharon to get home, I ordered Chinese food from a restaurant not far from my house. I got my usual beef and broccoli and Sharon the General Tso chicken. We have been to many Chinese restaurants in Philly, and I even had an academic conference in Hangzhou, China, and Sharon came with me. We tried some exciting dishes while there, none of which tasted anything like what we get in the US, but they were still enjoyable.

We usually have wine with our Chinese food, but I decided that beer was probably best tonight. We have been in a bit of a rut with the wine of late. We loved Hoegaarden from Belgium, and I had a six-pack in the fridge. It seemed like the night was set.

Sharon walked in, and I could instantly tell that she was wiped. We did a little smack on the lips, and then she just flopped onto the couch.

I said, "That bad, huh?"

"It wasn't that bad of a day, but I've got a lot bouncing around in my head right now. Some weird things were going on with this case. How was your day?"

"Well, I'm sure you remember Emily Keen of the FBI from down at the Outer Banks. I contacted her today to get a referral for an agency that could help me with my case. I connected with her, and she was indeed able to help me out."

"I do remember her, and it's great that you were able to connect with her and that she would help. It sounds like you're making more progress than I am."

"How about we break out the Chinese food? I also thought we might switch to beer tonight. I've got Hoegaarden on the chill in the fridge. Maybe we can think of something to talk about other than work at least while we eat."

Sharon smiled and said, "Sounds like a decent plan to me, but we've both been working so much; I hope you have a topic other than work for conversation. I'm feeling pretty flat."

"Allow me to be the entertainment committee for the evening."

I spread out the food and beer on the dining room table. Got us some plates, silverware, and napkins. Maybe if I put a little effort into dinner, we could figure out something other than work to talk about.

I tried sports first. "So, you know that the Phillies have had a decent start to their season. Bryce Harper is already on a tear. Do you want to catch a game soon?"

"Sure. Always happy to head down to Citizen's Bank. We should get to a game sometime soon." Then she just returned to her food with her head down.

I figured I'd try vacation next. "Okay, I'll get the schedule, and we'll pick a game. Since we're talking about getting out of the house, any place, in particular, you would like to try for vacation this year? I don't have any conferences on the horizon right now, so we can just head out wherever we like."

Sharon looked up from her food and said, "I don't know. We've been traveling a lot lately, so I'm not sure I want to go on another quest. Maybe something a little more local."

"Well, we haven't just gone down to the Jersey shore for a week of hanging at the beach in a while. Want to just head down to Cape May and kick back on the beach?"

"That sounds pretty nice. A little decompress time would be great." Again, she just looked down at her food and seemed preoccupied.

"Okay, I've tried for distraction, but you have something important on your mind. Just FYI, I will look for some Cape May places, but go ahead and give me a rundown on what happened today.

"That obvious, huh? Okay, overall, the case is going as I would have expected. Clearly, the victim was tortured, but we don't know why it happened. The guy had a small jewelry store and probably made a decent living, but it doesn't look like anything was taken from the store. Maybe he had a load of cash somewhere in the store, but that doesn't explain the torture. The assailants would only torture the victim to extract some sort of information that was not easily accessible. The ME and CSI folks don't have evidence of what the torturers would want from this guy. But that's not what is bugging me right now."

"I'm ready. Give it to me!"

"I can't put my finger right on it, but the father-in-law is sending a tingle down my spine that somehow he is involved."

"You mean you think a little ultra-Orthodox Jewish guy is somehow involved with a torture/murder incident? As you know, your instincts have been right on in several cases I've been involved in, but this seems a bit of a stretch. Are you sure you're not just looking for any angle that might help?"

"It's a valid question, and I can't guarantee that I have a reasonable response. Something seems fishy about the guy, but I admit that I have not been around ultra-Orthodox Jewry very much, so what I see as weird may be quite normal for that group. I was raised as a Reform Jew, so my view of Judaism and Jewish customs and rituals are light-years from the ultra-Orthodox sect. So, I may be looking for something when there isn't anything to find."

"Did you adhere to the family's request about releasing the body?"

"Released it at about 4 pm. The ME could have used a little more time, but he said he felt like he did a decent job. Not great, but decent."

"Well, at least that time pressure is off. From working with you on some cases, I know you will still have to continue gathering evidence in a hurry because the trail can get cold quickly, but at least you won't have the guy's family standing over you."

"That's my problem right now. I know the family has five more days of shiva to sit, but no one seems interested in finding the murderer or murderers. The wife had no problem giving us an extra day, but the father-in-law seemed reluctant to do that. This is where my lack of Jewish education is a hindrance."

I suddenly had what I thought was a good idea. "Maybe you need to get some ultra-Orthodox advice. Why don't you find out if anyone at the station knows Orthodox adherents? I doubt you have any ultra-Orthodox Jews on the force, but surely someone knows someone who follows the Orthodox faith. I read there are over 200,000 Jews in the Philly area, so there's got to be someone who can help."

Sharon smiled for the first time that evening. She said, "I don't know why I didn't think of that, but that's a great idea. And I know a couple of Jewish guys on the force who are pretty religious, so they may be able to help. Thanks so much for the advice." She leaned over and gave me a hard kiss on the mouth. "So, do you want to talk about your day? Maybe I can provide you with a breakthrough, too."

"You might actually do that, but after that kiss you just gave me, I'm willing to postpone the debrief of my day if we can find something else for entertainment tonight."

She leaned over the table and started to unbutton her dress. She just smiled as she continued.

I said, "Yep, that works."

# Chapter Fourteen

Josef's and Risa's shul members had all been paying their respects while the family had been sitting shiva. Josef had felt tremendous guilt that he had helped directly in Lev's death. He tried to convince himself that it wasn't his fault since he hadn't wanted Lev to be killed. But deep in his heart, he knew that wasn't true. He started the ball rolling, and it quickly got out of hand. Nevertheless, he had to show the proper remorse when people called.

One man Josef knew very well from the shul was Isak Zylberman. Josef also knew that Isak's daughter, Raisa, had been trying to divorce her husband for some time, but similar to Lev, he had been unwilling to give her a get. Josef knew that Isak was getting very frustrated with his son-in-law, so maybe Josef could satisfy the Russian mobsters by putting Isak in touch with them.

When Isak and Raisa came to the house, they sat with Risa and the rest of the family for a good while. When Josef went to the kitchen, Isak decided to follow him.

Isak told Josef, "I'm very sorry for your loss, but at least Risa is through with that jerk, Lev. I've heard that he had been a hard case on the get Risa wanted. Same thing I'm going through with my deadbeat son-in-law, David. At least Lev was willing to work and had a thriving business. David doesn't want to work and expects me to foot the bill for him and his family. I doubt he loves Raisa, but he certainly loves not having to work. Lazy bum!"

Josef nodded and hesitated before he replied. He knew he was probably only digging deeper in a hole if he gave Isak a contact with the Russians, but he felt he probably had to give them something to get them off his back.

"Isak, I probably shouldn't tell you this, but I know a way you may be able to get what you want as far as a divorce."

"Really! That would be great. I've offered the guy as much money as I could gather, but he won't budge. I think he's afraid he'd just blow through whatever money I gave him, and then he might have to work. What do you have in mind?"

Josef was choking a bit, but he said, "I know a couple of Russian guys who might be able to encourage David to sign the get."

It didn't take long for Isak to try to put it together. "You mean you paid some Russians to murder Lev?"

"No, that is not what I did, and this doesn't involve me. I've just heard through the grapevine that some Russians are good at achieving results with this particular issue." Josef turned his head. "Maybe we should forget the whole thing. Never mind that I even mentioned it."

Isak took Josef's shoulder and turned it so Josef faced him. "Josef, I don't need to know anything about what you did or didn't do. None of my business. But, if you know how I can get this bum of a husband out of Raisa's life, I would greatly appreciate your assistance."

Josef knew that he was now at a crossroads. He either had to give Isak a name or risk that somehow Isak made some contact with the mob on his own, and they found out Josef had not offered their services. He was in a very tight spot, with no easy way out, but he decided to trust Isak.

"I can give you the name and number of a Russian guy who will help meet your needs. All I'm going to do is give you the name and number. What happens after that is none of my business."

Isak had a slight grin on his face. He felt he knew exactly what Josef had done and didn't care. He was just as desperate as Josef was, so he nodded and said, "Give me the info, and we will never again speak on this topic."

Josef took out a piece of paper and wrote the name of Leonid and a phone number. He handed it to Isak. Isak glanced at it and reached to shake Josef's hand. As they exchanged a brief handshake, Isak said, "Thank you, Josef. And if she knew, I'm sure Raisa would thank you, too." With that chat, Isak returned to the living room.

Josef stood in the kitchen and felt he might have just signed another guy's death warrant. All he could do was hope that David wasn't as stubborn as Lev.

After he left Risa's house, Isak went straight home. He sat in his den thinking about what he should do. He had the name and number right before him, but he was starting to have second thoughts. What would happen if the cops somehow put Lev's murder with his effort to get David to agree to a get? It seemed to be getting riskier and riskier.

Just at that moment, David came into the house. Isak said to him, "Have you gone over to pay your respects to Risa yet?"

"Nope, and I don't plan to. I never liked Lev that much; the guy worked too hard and never had any fun. He was always at that damn jewelry store, day and night."

"He was trying to provide for his family, as any respectable man would. He may not have been the best husband to Risa, but he was a good breadwinner."

"So what? I've always thought that part of the reason to get married is so your in-laws can give you a good life. Marriage includes being provided for."

Isak was angry and said, "And what part of the Talmud told you that your in-laws are responsible for providing for you? I must have missed that part when I was a Talmudic student."

"I guess you did. The part says the wife will do whatever the husband wants, including getting her father to provide for her husband. I can't tell you the exact chapter, but I know it's in there."

"No, there is a lot in the Talmud, but I'm sure there is nothing there about supporting a son-in-law who decides to be a lazy bum."

David snickered and said, "Well, it says so in my reading. Why the hell do you think I married your frumpy daughter? You didn't think I could do better? Many better-looking women were out there, but their fathers didn't earn enough to provide for my needed lifestyle. So, I ended up stuck with Raisa. Man has to do what a man has to do."

With that, he waived to Isak and upstairs.

Isak stood for just a second, fuming. Then he went into his den and closed the door. He took out the paper and started to punch in the number. It was time to get that jerk out of his life, whatever it took.

# Chapter Fifteen

Sharon was again up early, but she told me to stay in bed. She made a pot of coffee, put some in a thermos she had, kissed me on the forehead, and told me to have a good day.

She headed straight to the stationhouse as she wanted to try to talk to a fellow detective named Samuel Bernstein. She knew that Bernstein was more religious than she was and that he might provide some guidance or assistance in finding someone in the Orthodox community who would be able to give her some ideas about why Josef might be acting the way he was.

Once she got to the office, she looked up Bernstein's extension and gave him a buzz. After two rings, he answered, "Detective Bernstein."

"Sam. It's Sharon Levin over in homicide. How are you doing?"

"Good to hear from you, Sharon. I'm doing okay. Got a B&E job from over on the Boulevard on my plate right now. Why, whatcha got?"

"Sam, I know this will sound weird, but I need some help with an Orthodox Jewish question. I thought I knew that you were more observant than I am."

Sam chuckled, "From what I know of you, Sharon, if I had bagels and cream cheese regularly, I would be more observant than you are. But you should know I'm not Orthodox; I follow Conservative traditions."

"Do you know anything about the Orthodox community here in Philadelphia?"

Sam said, "Actually, I know a little. One of my buddies decided to move from Orthodox to Conservative Judaism, and we've talked about why he did it. Why? What's going on? Is it about the Orthodox guy who was tortured and killed? I heard about it from the scuttlebutt around the station."

"Yep, that's what it's about. Any chance I can buy you a cup of coffee at the Starbucks around the corner? If no Starbucks, I have a thermos I brought from home."

"Believe it or not, I like the coffee at the stationhouse. Why don't I grab a cup and head to your office?"

"See you in a few minutes."

Sam walked into Sharon's office about five minutes later. They shook hands, and Sam took the guest chair. "So, I'm going to tell you that I'm not an expert on ultra-Orthodox Judaism, but what's on your mind?"

"Since you've already heard about the torture and murder aspect, I won't bore you with that. And you probably know that we're just getting started on the investigation, but something is already weird. I met with the father-in-law of the murdered guy, and it doesn't seem like he cares if we find the culprit who killed his son-in-law. I know that there are strict rules about Jewish burials, but this guy seems more interested in getting his son-in-law buried than finding his murderer."

"Well, I know that there are some very stringent rules on burials and that time is of the essence. But I would think that with a murder, there would be some flexibility."

"That's what's weird! The guy's wife was willing to allow the ME some time to do his thing, but the father-in-law pushed to get the guy buried. He gave the ME only one extra day to do the autopsy. The ME thinks he still did a decent job, but he could have done better with a little more time. He did find out that the victim was an Ashkenazi Jew."

"Interesting. So, what do you want me to do?"

"Any chance you know any ultra-Orthodox rabbis? I think I might be missing something about Jewish burial rules, and a rabbi might provide some insight on the subject."

"Funny you should mention that. I do know an ultra-Orthodox rabbi. It's not through my Conservative Jewish buddy, but the rabbi helped me with a burglary case about a year ago. Someone broke into a Jewish deli and stole the money they had stored in a safe in the back. Whoever did it went to a lot of trouble to break in. I discussed who would know about the money in the safe with the rabbi. I knew he was tapped into the ultra-Orthodox Jewish community, so I figured he might be able to help."

"Did he?"

"Not really. He told me that the ultra-Orthodox community was very loyal to one another, so he doubted it was part of that group. He gave me a couple of Russian-Jewish guys who were known to be hooked into the mob. I hauled them in for questioning, but nothing panned out. We never cleared the case."

"Think the rabbi would talk to me about my question?"

"Let me go back to my office, look up his number and give him a call. I'll let you know." With that, Bernstein left Sharon's office.

While waiting for Bernstein to get back to her, she reviewed the ME report again. She didn't see anything new. All that jumped out was how badly this guy had been treated. Whatever the murderers wanted from him must have been very important. She just couldn't figure out what that might be.

Sharon's phone rang; she picked it up, and it was Bernstein. He said, "So I spoke to this ultra-Orthodox rabbi who said he would be willing to talk to you. His name is Rabbi Efim Shulman. His number is 215-546-2768. He's waiting for your call."

"Thanks a lot for the help, Sam. If you ever decide to upgrade to Starbucks, it's on me."

Sharon dialed the number, and it was immediately answered. "Rabbi Shulman."

"Rabbi, my name is Sharon Levin. My colleague, Samuel Bernstein, just hung up with you. I wondered if you have some time to talk briefly with me about a murder case I have."

"Ms. Levin, I just read in the papers that Lev Brodsky was murdered, and it's a tragedy. If fact, he and his family are members of our congregation. I was at their home helping them sit shiva earlier today. I'm not sure I know how I can help, but if you want to come over to my temple, I'll help if I can."

"Do you have any time now?"

"Actually, I do. My shul is over on Castor Avenue. I can give you a little time."

"On my way, and thank you."

Sharon knew where the ultra-Orthodox synagogue was on Castor, and it only took her a few minutes to get there. She parked in the lot out front, went to the door, and knocked.

A gray-haired gentleman opened the door. His hair had lengthy payos curls, and his beard was long. He wore ultra-Orthodox black clothing with a hat that looked like a fedora. He introduced himself, "I'm Rabbi Shulman. Please come in."

Sharon knew that ultra-Orthodox men do not make physical contact with women other than their wives, so she did not extend her hand. She followed the rabbi into what she guessed must have been his office.

He said, "Please sit down. I can only offer you water to drink as that is all I have available."

Sharon said, "I'm fine. Thank you for seeing me.

"I'm not sure how I can help, but Lev's family has always been very involved in our community, and his death is a great loss. What can I help you with?"

"Rabbi, I will just get straight to the point. As you may or may not know, Lev wasn't just murdered; he was tortured beforehand."

"I didn't know that. Obviously, I knew he had been killed, but I did not know those circumstances. That is just terrible news."

"Yes, it is. However, I wanted to ask you about Lev's father-in-law, Josef Goldstein."

"Josef has been a prominent member of our shul for many years. I'm sure he's devastated by his son-in-law's death."

Sharon replied, "Actually, that's what I came to ask you about. At least on the surface, he doesn't seem devastated at all. In fact, he doesn't seem that interested in finding out who killed Lev. He just wants to get Lev buried, sit for the requisite shiva time, and then just move on. Lev's wife, Risa, seems much more interested in finding the killer than Josef."

"That is very strange. Josef has lost other family members and has gone to great links to provide for a proper burial. Josef is always the first man to offer his time to form a minyan when someone dies in our community. I consider him very observant even by our standards, which I'm sure you know are pretty high."

Sharon said, "I do know that, which is why his behavior is somewhat troubling. What I know of the ultra-Orthodox community seems out of sorts, even though I don't know Josef. Has there been anything unusual happening with Josef lately? I don't know, does he seem like himself to you."

By Shulman's facial expression, Sharon could tell that she had struck a nerve on something. She sat and waited to see if Shulman would offer any explanation. Finally, after almost a minute, Shulman said, "We don't discuss personal matters within our community with outsiders."

"So, I take it from that comment that something happened involving Josef, Lev, or both. Rabbi, I'm trying to solve a murder here and bring some comfort to the Brodsky family. I'm also doing my job, so I would be very grateful if you have any insights that might help me do that job."

Shulman sat for a minute and looked out the window behind his chair. Finally, he said with his back to Sharon, "Lev and Risa have been having many marital problems for some time."

"People go through marital issues. It's certainly not that unusual. I'm sure even ultra-Orthodox Jews have marital problems. They're still humans."

"Yes, but marital issues within the ultra-Orthodox community are much more complicated than the norm. Do you know what a get is?"

"I know it's a part of getting a divorce, but not much more than that."

"As you probably know, the ultra-Orthodox faith provides that men are the head of any household. Women take secondary roles.

For our current discussion, if a woman wants to divorce a man, the man must agree to the divorce by signing a document. The get."

"And I take it Risa has wanted to divorce Lev, but he was unwilling to sign the get."

Shulman turned back to Sharon with his head down. He said, "Yes, without going into details about why she wanted a divorce; Risa has been trying to obtain the get for over a year. Josef had offered Lev money, even part of his business, but Lev was unwilling to sign the document. Even though he no longer loved Risa, he felt it would be embarrassing to get a divorce. He was willing to live in an unhappy marriage rather than having the shame of divorce on him. I tried to convince him that his happiness was more important than staying with a woman he no longer loved, but he was obstinate."

"Rabbi, that info certainly sheds some new light on the investigation, but I'm not sure where to go with it."

Shulman responded, "Since I've told you this much already, I might as well give you the rest. Josef told me he was furious with Lev about not signing the get. He told me he would do anything to get his lovely Risa away from Lev. Anything at all."

Sharon sat and thought: Anything at all covers a lot of ground. It sounded like she might finally have a real clue about this case.

# Chapter Sixteen

Isak sat at a table in the café where he was supposed to meet the guy who would fix the situation with David. Since Isak was the only one dressed in ultra-Orthodox clothing in the restaurant, it would be easy to pick him out.

Again, right before he made the call, Isak started having second thoughts. He went through all the negative possibilities that could happen. While he hated David's laziness, he knew it bothered Raisa much less. Isak wasn't sure that Raisa still loved David, but she was more willing to tolerate him than Risa was with Lev. He knew it was perilous to use these mobster guys so soon after Lev's murder, but his anger towards David had reached a new level. Calling his beautiful daughter frumpy to his face had been the final nail. As nervous as he was about this whole thing, he could not bring himself to tolerate such disrespect. Something had to be done.

As Isak debated his situation, two somewhat scary-looking men walked through the door. They headed straight to Isak's table. The taller one said, "You're Isak, right?"

Isak started to stand, but the taller guy waved for him to sit. The guy said, "I'm Leonid. He's Mikhail. We hear you might have a family issue we can help with."

Isak instantly regretted this idea. Both of these guys looked like they would not hesitate for a second to kill someone. Beating a guy would be like a holiday for them. Isak said, "Actually, I think I have changed my mind. I'm sorry to have brought you out for nothing. I would happily buy you lunch or something as payment for your valuable time."

Leonid and Mikhail turned to each other and smiled. Mikhail said, "I don't think you understand. You called us, and we came. Essentially, we already have a deal. The only thing we need to negotiate is the deal's terms."

"How could we already have a deal? We've only met and spoken to each other for less than five minutes. As I said, I would be happy to buy you lunch, but I don't want to engage your services."

Leonid said, "You engaged our services when you called. You've now seen our faces and know our first names. You could easily call the cops and perhaps create some aggravation for us. The way that we prevent that is to consecrate a deal so we all have some skin in the game."

Now Isak was starting to sweat. He said, "How much must I pay you for you just to walk away?"

Mikhail replied, "See, that's the problem. If you just give us the money we demand, you will not have broken any laws. In fact, you could turn us in quite quickly to the cops. We need you to be on the hook for a crime to keep your mouth shut once you pay us. So, you should tell us what you want to be done, and we'll tell you how much to pay. I'm afraid just changing your mind and walking away will not happen."

Isak now knew he was in big trouble. "I will give you whatever you want, just to leave me alone."

"You're still not getting it," said Leonid. "Yes, we could take your money and threaten you to keep your mouth shut, but you still won't have committed a crime. Plus, you might as well let us take care of whatever problem you have because our fee is $100,000."

Isak almost choked! One hundred thousand dollars! He didn't have that kind of money. As the head meat cutter for the largest kosher butcher in Philly, he did reasonably well, but he didn't have that kind of money at his disposal. He said, "Gentlemen, I don't have that kind of money. I'm just a meat cutter. I'm not rich."

Leonid leaned in and said, "Your friend, Josef, said he couldn't find the money either, and yet he did. It's amazing how quickly you can raise money if properly motivated. And, so that you know, we can certainly get you properly motivated. Anyway, give us a quick rundown on what you called us to do."

Isak felt he was stuck right now. He wanted to excuse himself and run out of the café, but he didn't see that ending well for him. So, he said, "My daughter is married to a lazy jerk who basically lives off my family. He doesn't want to work, and he never really has. He used to help in the markets, but he decided it was easier to just live off of me. I think my daughter would divorce him if he offered her a get."

Mikhail smiled and said, "But I take it he's not ready to do that, and you would like us to encourage him to do it."

"Yes, that is why I called you when Josef gave me your number. But I don't want him killed. I want him to ask Raisa for a divorce and offer her a get. Again, I think she will take it if he offers."

"So, you assume that we are responsible for Lev's demise," said Leonid.

"I know nothing about what happened to Lev, I swear. But I do know that he was murdered, and as much as I hated him, I don't want my son-in-law killed. Plus, I think that would make the police even more suspicious and might cause all of us some trouble."

Mikhail said, "Without admitting to anything, we can assure you that your son-in-law won't be killed but that he will be happy to give your daughter what she wants. We need 25,000 dollars upfront and the balance when the job is done."

"But I told you I don't have that kind of money. I'm only a lowly meat cutter."

"That's your problem," said Leonid. "Just find the 25K first, then give us the remaining 75K after the job. As I said, Josef also felt he had cash flow problems, but once we enlightened him about what happens if we don't get paid, he rounded up the money. Actually, the final installment was in gold and jewelry, which ended up being worth more than the cash. Amazing what motivated people can accomplish."

Isak said, "You'll have to give me some time to raise the funds. I don't have that kind of money sitting around."

"We'll give you two days to find the first 25K. We will expect to hear from you within that timeframe. Otherwise, we may have to encourage other family members, including your beloved daughter. You understand?"

Isak nodded his head. He understood all too well. Like Josef, he had just signed a deal with the devil!

# Chapter Seventeen

While Sharon returned to her office to start evaluating what to do with Rabbi Shulman's information, I was in my office at Temple, spending some time on my analysis of Brownstein and Williams. It was only 2 pm, and I had my only class of the day at 6 pm, so I had some time to look at things.

The information I got from Mikayla at FinCEN really told a compelling story. I had looked at some of her reports, and it was abundantly clear that Petrovsky Markets was laundering some cash. The question was, of course, whose cash?

Since Petrovsky was a Russian-owned company, it seemed likely that the Russian mob was somehow involved. In the papers, I read about how the mob had infiltrated some major US cities, including New York, Boston, and Philadelphia. According to numerous reports, the mob was involved in drugs, racketeering, extortion, and all the usual enterprises. Naturally, they had a lot of cash they needed to launder. From my experience in New Orleans, I knew that casinos were a ripe place to move the cash, and there were plenty of casinos in the Philly area and a ton down in Atlantic City. But the Casino Control Divisions in both PA and NJ were actually pretty decent. They were naturally far from perfect but better than many locales. Indeed, a lot better than some of the overseas casinos, like in Macau, where the cash funnels through the system with ease. But most mobsters want multiple means of laundering their cash, and using small businesses was very popular.

While I wanted to examine Petrovsky Markets more closely, I wasn't sure about any other Brownstein and Williams clients. The PCAOB only examines accounting firms that deal primarily in public, not private companies. Petrovsky is a relatively small company, and not publicly traded. However, Brownstein and Williams have about a dozen small publicly-traded firms they audit. During a previous PCAOB audit that focused on publicly traded companies, Petrovsky came up for review. It had hit the PCAOB radar because it appeared to be pouring a good deal of money into a small tech company, TechSounds, set up in West Philadelphia. Two computer science students from Drexel and Penn started TechSounds. Its purpose was to record music at various concert venues in the area, and then make that music available online for a fee. Though only in their 20s, the two founders had become Grateful Dead fans and saw how much of the live Dead music was traded around the internet now. The founders approached several local music venues, like City Winery, for permission to record some of their artists. By going through the appropriate systems, they could record the music but not to worry about being sued for copyright infringement. Any artist who appeared at one of the venues legally agreed that TechSounds could record the concert.

TechSounds had decided to ride the internet music wave of Spotify and iTunes but with live music recently recorded. When they first started, TechSounds just looked like another internet idea going to go bust, but then they caught a break. One of the heads of a venture capital firm in downtown Philly, John Flannigan, happened to be a huge Dead fan. He was constantly trolling the internet looking for Dead music that he didn't have. While TechSounds didn't have any Dead music available, during his search, Flannigan found TechSounds. He wasn't sure that the business idea was that sound, but when he approached the two students, it was clear they didn't need that much of an investment to get it moving. He fronted them one million dollars, and they went public and had slowly been building their sales and profits.

Since I'm a big music fan, the general idea of TechSounds appealed to me. Still, when I pulled up their publicly available financial statements, it was hard to figure out if they were making any money or not. But I knew from experience that was the way many startups look early on. But the big question was why

Petrovsky was devoting so much money to TechSounds at this early stage of development. Maybe it was just money, but TechSounds being public had provided the PCAOB with a reason to examine Petrovsky.

The previous PCAOB review highlighted some small issues Brownstein and Williams needed to fix to comply fully. They had addressed most of them, but they had avoided doing anything about Petrovsky since it is a private company. I decided what the hell, and I would talk to one of the managing partners at Brownstein and Williams using the guise of TechSounds, but eventually getting around to Petrovsky. Even if TechSounds was solid on the surface, things could still be a little murkier if you drill down a little further, including a look at Petrovsky. Since it seemed like Sharon would be busy for a while, I felt like doing a little drilling.

I looked up the phone number of Brownstein and Williams. Time to rattle a few accounting cages.

# Chapter Eighteen

Isak deeply regretted his decision to contact the Russian mob about getting his son-in-law to give his daughter a get. He kept telling himself that he should have known better. He had relatives who lived in Israel and heard the stories of how the Russian mob who had immigrated there operated. Even including the Israeli intelligence service, the Mossad, the Israeli government had tried to reign in the Russian mobsters for many years. They had had some successes, but the mob still had a significant presence in that country. And he had heard some of the stories about mob activity in the US, particularly in New York City. He should have known that this whole thing was a bad idea, but now that it has started, he didn't really how to get out of it.

One of his biggest mistakes was not asking Raisa how she felt her marriage to David was going. Certainly, Isak saw how they were together in the house, and while there didn't seem to be tremendous animosity between them, there also didn't seem to be much love. They just seemed to be existing.

He had decided he needed to talk to Raisa and find out how she felt about David. Such a discussion was unusual for Orthodox Jews, but he thought he had to know if he was letting his dislike of David color what Raisa thought of David. If Raisa still loved David, then Isak would give the mob the money they demanded and write it off. He kicked himself again for not gauging Raisa's feelings for David before he contacted the mob. All he could do now was find out if this whole idea was even worth the effort and money.

He had set up 3 pm as a time for Raisa and him to talk. He had told her it was about something at the synagogue, and she assumed it was about Lev and Risa. At 3 pm, the two of them met in the dining room. Raisa had made coffee, offered some to Isak, and the two of them sat.

"So, what are we talking about, Father?" inquired Raisa. "Something to do with Lev's murder, I guess?"

"Actually, no. What I want to discuss is likely to make you feel uncomfortable, so I wanted to warn you of that."

"Something uncomfortable? What could you possibly have on your mind that will make me uncomfortable?"

Isak replied, "I want to know how your marriage is going with David. Are you happy?"

"Of course, I'm happy. David and I have been married for almost fifteen years and have two wonderful kids. What could possibly make you think that I'm not happy?"

"I just don't see you two showing a lot of affection for each other."

"I will admit that David is not the most demonstrative husband in the world, but he has generally been very loving to me."

"Generally?"

"Okay, Dad, I will acknowledge that I would like David to work more and contribute to the household more. I know it bothers you immensely, and I have tried to convince David that he should find another job, pretty much any, but he still thinks it's his choice as the head of our household."

Isak could feel the anger starting to rage in his stomach. "But, Raisa, he's not the head of the household where he lives: I am! Yes, I know you and David had your own house for many years, but you've been in my house since he decided last year that he didn't like to work. Doesn't any of David's friends make him feel embarrassed that he doesn't work?"

"They do, and Rabbi Shulman has come down on him pretty hard. But I just think David is going through a period of finding himself. Once he does, I think he'll rejoin the workforce."

Isak thought to himself: I wonder how long that will be. He asked Raisa, "And do you know how long it will take him to find himself?"

"No, I don't. I hope that it doesn't take too long because I know we are putting a strain on your income by David not working. If you want, I'll talk to him about it."

"You shouldn't have to talk to him. He should want to provide for his family. If he's going to put himself up as the head of his household, he needs to act like someone who deserves that position. And I think he should show you more affection since you have been his loyal wife while he has been finding himself."

"I do wish he was more inclined to work. I know you think he is just lazy. And I wish that he was more affectionate towards me." She lowered her eyes and said softly, "And less affectionate to others."

"What does that mean?" Isak said in a loud voice.

"Nothing. I was just talking out loud."

"No, you weren't just talking out loud. What the hell does that comment mean?"

"It's nothing. Don't worry about it."

"I'm going to worry about it, and you'll tell me what you mean. Has David been unfaithful to you?"

Raisa's eyes started to tear up, and she looked down towards the floor even more. She said softly, "I don't know if this is true or not, but someone at the shul said that David had a brief affair last year with a woman from our synagogue."

Isak's face instantly got very red. He yelled, "He did what? Who told you this?"

"Just a woman from the shul. I don't want to say whom. She said that she had heard David had been seeing a woman during the day when he was supposed to be working. In fact, that is why he lost his job?"

"He lost his job! He told us that he had quit because he didn't feel like working right now. He never said anything about being fired."

Raisa started to cry and said, "I knew I shouldn't have told you anything. I'm not even sure that it's true. It was just a rumor going around the shul."

"You're telling me other community members think he has been having an affair?"

"A few people have heard, but no one knows for sure again."

Isak yelled and said, "And why didn't you tell me? Did you talk to Rabbi Shulman about it?"

"No, father. I would be too ashamed to say anything to anybody if it is true. Our synagogue is very tightly knit, and I would not want the embarrassment imposed on our family. Besides, I'm sure it's over, even if it was true. David rarely leaves the house these days except to go to the market and services. He has no time to be involved with anyone."

"I can't believe you never told your mother or me about this. This accusation brings great shame to our family name. But more importantly, why are you still with this jerk? How can you stand to even be in the same room as he is, much less share a bed with him?"

"Father, I know I am not the most attractive ultra-Orthodox woman in the area. David is handsome, so he would have no problem finding a better-looking woman to be with. I don't want to become a spinster, plus I would need his permission to divorce him, and since you are providing him with an income, I doubt very much that he would grant me a get."

Isak thought again to himself: We'll see about that!

# Chapter Nineteen

I was almost home from my night class and wanted to check in on Sharon. In fact, I had tried to call and then text her, but no response yet. Guess she really has something important cooking tonight. I'm sure I'll get a rundown when she gets home.

Just at that moment, my phone rang with her ring tone. I hit the accept key and said, "Hey, you're a hard gal to get ahold of."

"Sorry. Been a busy day. However, I think I've made a little progress on my case. I'll tell you about it when I get home. How was your day at the office?"

"Not bad. I think I might have moved the needle a bit on my project, too. Why don't we save it until you get here? What do you want for dinner? Want me to cook something up?"

Sharon said, "Nah, it's late for you, too, so let's just get some takeout. If I weren't so tired, I would say we should break out of our takeout rut and actually go out, but I'm pretty beat."

"Well, we can break out of our rut a little by getting Indian food. I haven't had it in a while, and there's an Indian restaurant up the street called Rangoli that we've never tried. I could pull up the menu on my computer and give you a rundown of its choices."

"No need. You know what I like, and I'm sure they have some of those things. But it sounds like a great idea. Just don't get mine too spicy. I know you like to sweat when you have Indian."

I chuckled and said, "Fine, I will surprise you. Samosas to get us started?"

"You know me so well. We still have some Hoegaarden, don't we?"

"Yep, Indian food and Belgian beer. Perfect combo."

"See you in about 30 minutes."

I got the menu for Rangoli and looked at the choices. I knew Sharon loved Chicken Tikka Biryani, and I've always been a fan of Channa Masala. Why look any further? I called and placed the order, including Vegetable Samosa. They told me to pick it up in 20 minutes. That was perfect timing for when Sharon was to arrive.

Since I had a few minutes to kill, I decided to ponder what I was going to say to Arnold Brownstein, the managing partner at his firm. I had called and set up an appointment for tomorrow afternoon. He sounded like a pretty decent guy, and he didn't seem flustered when I told him I had some questions concerning the PCAOB review.

He told me he was happy to help in any way he could. He said that his firm takes its PCAOB obligations very seriously, so he was sure he could provide me with whatever information I needed. Of course, he wasn't going to say: Yeah, you caught us!

I knew I could ask him about TechSounds and why it seemed that Petrovsky was advancing so much cash. But that wasn't enough or a reason to ding his firm under PCAOB guidelines. I had to focus on Petrovsky Markets and the excess money that was flowing through the company. The problem was that Brownstein was the managing partner and didn't actually do the audit. He just signed the forms where they needed to be signed. However, ultimately, the audit was his responsibility as the partner-in-charge. Still, I was pretty sure that all I was going to get was that he would have his accounting staff look into the issue. That was, of course, unless he was part of the money-laundering scheme himself. Maybe that was the angle to take with him. Push him on his involvement and see if I can get a reaction.

It was time to go fetch the Indian food. It was a short walk, and when I went into the restaurant, I was overwhelmed with the great odors of an Indian place. We both loved Indian food, and it was great that there was one close by.

I picked up the food and walked back to my house. I saw Sharon parking just as I walked up. "Great timing," I said. I leaned forward and gave her a smack on the lips.

"Yes, it is. I'm starving and looking forward to some exotic food and beer. Maybe I'll spring for and even be dessert."

"I'll believe when it happens."

I entered the dining room and laid out some dishes, silverware, and glasses. Then I went to the fridge and got the beer. I found a bottle opener and poured a glass for both of us. Normally we would just eat out of the carryout box and beer bottle, but it seemed to me that we both had had pretty difficult days, so we deserved something a little nicer. I handed Sharon her food, and we started to prepare our plates.

Sharon said, "So do you want to talk about the Phillies or something or just jump right into work?"

"Phillies will only take us so far, so why don't we debrief on our days? You can go first."

"Well, building on your sage advice, I hooked up with a conservative Jewish guy from work, Sam Bernstein. He works burglary mostly. He said he would help me try to find an ultra-Orthodox rabbi who might know something about the victim and his family. He made a couple of calls and hooked me up with a Rabbi Efim Shulman, who actually was able to work me in for a quick meeting. The rabbi sort of toed the party line at first. Lev and Risa were great members of his shul. Lev was a hard worker at his store. Nothing helpful until, at the very end of the discussion, he admitted that Lev and Risa had been having problems and that the father, Josef, had become very angry with Lev of late. That explains why he hasn't seemed that upset that his son-in-law was murdered. Not sure it helps my case that much. At first, when he told me that, I was quite excited, but I tried to piece it together on the drive home, and I'm not sure what I got."

I said, "At least you're making some progress." Just then, a thought hit me. "You remember that episode of the Sopranos we watched when Tony cut a deal with an ultra-Orthodox Jewish guy in which Tony would get the guy's son-in-law to sign a divorce document? Silvio and Paulie threatened the guy with castration."

"I do. It's called a get. But it was also just a TV show. A good one, but still a TV show."

I replied, "That's true, but I remember there was an actual case up in New York where a rabbi was doling out harsh punishments to force ultra-Orthodox guys to sign gets they didn't want to sign. The press started calling the guy "The Prodfather" because he had boasted that he used cattle prods to convince guys to sign. I'm pretty sure the FBI set up a sting operation, and several guys, including at least one rabbi, went to jail."

"I do seem to remember a bit about that. Wasn't it back in the late 1990s into 2000? Wait, I see where you're headed. Could it be that Josef somehow got involved with mobsters to get Lev to sign a get?"

"Well, if the rabbi said that Lev and Risa were having problems, and you've seen that Josef doesn't seem too upset with Lev's demise, maybe it's something to consider."

"You know, you're a pretty decent detective for an accounting professor."

"Been hanging around you for a long time. Some of it had to brush off."

"Yeah, but none of your accounting brilliance has rubbed off on me yet."

"You have other enticing attributes that are much more valuable than learning how debits and credits work."

Sharon leaned over and kissed my hand. She said, "Since you have come up with a fascinating theory to help my case, unless you're dying to tell me what you found out today, we could finish dinner and move to the dessert, wink, wink, portion of the evening."

"Finishing my Channa Masala right now!"

# Chapter Twenty

After finding out about David's betrayal of his daughter, it didn't take Isak long to decide to go through with his original plan with the Russians. He still wasn't sure how he could round up the total fee of $100,000, but he did have an idea of how to put together the down payment of 25 large. Isak contacted Leonid and told him that he would have the money in three days. Leonid wasn't initially pleased about the time delay, but Isak reminded Leonid that he had given Isak two days to find the down payment, and he was only one day late, so he was doing the best he could. Leonid still wasn't happy, but he said he expected the money tomorrow.

While Isak was busy rounding up the money he needed, I was on my way to meet with the managing partner, Arnold Brownstein of Brownstein-Williams. Their offices were on the 35th floor of One Liberty Place on Market Street downtown. They were close enough to my house that I decided to walk versus a cab or Uber.

Having slept on it, I was now sure I would have to push Arnold some to get anything meaningful from him. I knew he had likely been through many IRS audits in addition to the PCAOB audit I knew about. It goes with the territory of having a CPA firm. Thus, I was pretty sure he was fast on his feet if he was being questioned hard on any topic. So, I was going to have to be very calm and composed, at least at the start, because if I came straight at him, I was sure he would respond with bluster, and I would get nowhere. And while I wasn't really on a tight clock to get this done, I knew the PCAOB folks would like to see my report sooner rather than later. Plus, I had begun to sense that there was much more going on here than just a bit of shoddy auditing. I just wasn't sure what it was.

When I arrived at Liberty Place, I took the elevator up to the 35th floor. When I exited, I saw that Brownstein-Williams took up the entire floor. I walked over to the reception desk, and the guy behind the desk said to me, "Welcome to Brownstein-Williams. How can I help you?"

"Good morning. My name is Dr. Ben Stone, and I have an appointment with Arnold Brownstein."

He said, "One moment, and I will check with his assistant."

Even though it was 2022, it still shocked me a bit when there was a guy in the receptionist's chair. Yeah, I knew I was showing my age a bit. And my girlfriend is a homicide cop, so I was sort of past the gender-role stereotypes, but the receptionist role still seemed to me like it should be a woman. Of course, if I ever said that to Sharon, I would be smacked in the mouth.

The receptionist hung up the phone and said, "Please have a seat, Dr. Stone. Mr. Brownstein's assistant will be out in a moment."

I took a seat and glanced around at the magazines they had. *The CPA Journal, Journal of Accountancy,* and *The Practical Accountant.* In short, the usual cast of characters. But they were still good solid practitioner journals. It wouldn't count for me at Temple because they weren't "academic" enough, but very useful to practicing CPAs.

As I sat there, I couldn't help but wonder if Brownstein's assistant would be a man. Maybe the firm has decided that men make better assistants. At that moment, a lovely blond came around the corner

She came over and stuck out her hand. As I returned her handshake, she said, "Dr. Stone. My name is Linda, and I am Mr. Brownstein's administrative assistant. Please follow me back to his office."

We passed a couple of suites with multiple people hunched over their computers. I assumed they were staff and managerial accountants. All the computers still seemed a bit funny to me.

When I started accounting, we still had thirteen-column worksheets spread over our desks. Things have sure changed.

We returned to what appeared to be a large office with an excellent desk for Linda to use. There was a guest chair off to the side. Linda said, "Mr. Brownstein is finishing up a phone call. He should only be a few more minutes. Please have a seat. Can I get you something to drink?"

"Thanks, but I'm fine," I replied.

I was only sitting in the chair for about five minutes before the large door behind Linda opened. A man about my size stepped out. Business casual had even hit the accounting profession. I couldn't tell if the guy was an accounting partner or headed to the golf course. Actually, he was probably doing both.

He extended his hand and said, "Dr. Stone. My name is Arnold Brownstein. Please call me Arnold."

I took his hand and said, "And please call me Ben."

"Please come into my office. By the way, did Linda offer you something to drink?"

"She did. I'm fine."

We went back into his office. It was undoubtedly more sprawling than my one at Temple. Massive, likely mahogany, desk. Big screen computer on that desk. The back wall had all of his degrees and professional certifications prominently displayed. The desk was elegant, but I expected that from an accounting partner.

He pointed to the overstuffed leather chair in front of his desk. He took his place behind the desk and sat in a similar chair. He started the conversation with, "So, Ben, I understand you are doing some consulting with the PCAOB, and you have some questions about our last review?"

"I do, but first of all, I wanted to assure you that my inquiries are really quite minimal. Your firm has done an excellent job filing all the appropriate documents for the PCAOB." I didn't really believe that, but I wanted to try to gain his trust.

"Ben, that is nice to hear, but to be honest, I wasn't too worried when you called and asked if we could meet. We take our obligations with the PCAOB very seriously, and I wasn't too concerned that you had something seriously amiss."

I thought to myself: What else was I expecting him to say? "There is only one of your clients that I need some clarification on TechSounds. However, if you know anything about a small company named Petrovsky Markets, that would be helpful, too."

Brownstein leaned back and smiled, "I am stunned. I certainly thought you would be interested in one or more of our larger clients. TechSounds is a small startup with straightforward accounting action. And Petrovsky Markets is also pretty tiny even to a firm our size. The only reason we keep them around is that my father grew up with the founder of Petrovsky Markets. They both went to high school together in Northeast Philly. Anyway, what can I try to answer for you?"

"Arnold, I'll just cut to the chase. I examined some of your PCAOB reports, and everything looked pretty clean. However, there were a couple of items that I thought needed some further investigation. As you noted, TechSounds is a small startup with about a million dollars in seed money. It's not my place to debate the soundness of their business strategy, but they seem to be doing pretty well regarding investments. What is a little strange is that Petrovsky Markets, according to the documents I have, has been investing heavily in TechSounds. I guess my first question is: Why would a Jewish market invest so much money in an internet startup?"

"To be honest with you, Ben, I don't know. As I'm sure you know, I don't do any of the actual auditing as a managing partner. I can certainly connect you with one of our senior auditors. I'm sure that person can give you some insight into why Petrovsky is investing as it is."

I replied, "That would be great. But the other main question is: How is Petrovsky so profitable that it can make these investments?" It's just three little markets in Northeast Philly, but it is pouring tons of cash into TechSounds. I've done enough audits and seen enough financial statements to wonder where the money is coming from. Any ideas?"

Brownstein's demeanor changed very quickly. "Well, as you probably know, small businesses deal a lot of cash. Sometimes that cash isn't reported properly. Naturally, we try to be as complete as possible with our examinations, but it's hard to catch all the cash transactions. If we had access to FinCEN, we could provide a much better picture of a firm's cash transactions. But we don't."

I decided it was time to pull the trigger. "Well, Arnold, I have access to FinCEN as part of my examination, and the story they found was quite illuminating. They tracked the cash transactions that went through Petrovsky's bank, First American, and a large number of deposits went through at just below the $10,000 threshold for reporting. Because of coming in below the threshold, the bank has never reported any unusual transactions. But it appears that Petrovsky is moving a lot of cash into the banking system, including TechSounds. As I'm sure you know, once the cash is in the financial system, the money can be moved anywhere."

Arnold's face changed from nervous to outright scared. He said, "Well, obviously, we only have banking records for the December yearend audit and tax return we do. We do not track the cash transactions for the entire year. We ensure that the cash reported at yearend reconciles with the yearend bank statement. We've never noticed any unusual activity for the yearend cash accounts."

Because you know that you only need the December statement to do the audit and tax return, I thought. And if you are involved with this scheme, you just tell Petrovsky to play it clean for December. I said, "Well, Arnold, I would have thought you would have wondered where all the Petrovsky investments in TechSounds come from. Petrovsky has invested a good deal of money in TechSounds. Certainly, more than three small markets would be able to do."

"As I said, I don't do the actual audits or even the tax returns. My main focus is practice development and getting and retaining clients. However, I'll give you the phone number of our senior auditor, Bill James, and you can set up an appointment with him. I am quite sure there is a reasonable explanation for what you've found, and I'm confident that Bill can provide you with that reasoning."

I was also quite confident Bill would have an explanation, but I was just wondering if it would be true!

# Chapter Twenty-One

While I was heading back to campus for a class, Sharon was busy doing some more research about the Russian mob in Philadelphia. She knew a lot about how the Russian mob operated, but the angle about the ultra-Orthodox divorce gets was news to her. She googled the facts of the case in New York and how there were similar situations that supposedly had occurred in Israel and other areas. There didn't seem to be a massive market for such services, but it certainly existed. Even though Sharon is not very religious, she was stunned that those activities were acceptable in the Jewish faith. But she knew she had to get closer to what might have happened. It was time to check in with her Jewish expert: Sam Bernstein.

She called Sam, and he picked up the phone. "Bernstein."

"Sam, it's Sharon. Are you busy right now? I have a couple of follow-up questions from my Jewish expert."

"I am far from an expert, but I may be more literate on Judaism than you are. Sure, I've got a little time. Want me to come up to your office?"

"That would be great. Still okay with the crappy coffee we have at the station?"

"Still works for me. I'm on my way."

Sam came straight up and came into Sharon's office. They said hello, and Sam took a seat. He said, "So do you need to know how to tolerate Gefilte fish? I would recommend a lot of horseradish."

Sharon smiled and said, "No, I'm good with Gefilte fish. I don't usually hit it very often. My question is about divorce gets again. Last night Ben told me a story about a group of ultra-

86

Orthodox people, including a rabbi in New York, who had tortured some men to get them to grant the gets that some daughters wanted. I was wondering if you knew anything about it."

"I saw the episode of the Sopranos, but that's all I know about it. I've heard a few rumors of things, but not much that I could confirm. Russian mob would probably be involved if something like that happened. You think something like the Sopranos show happened with the guy tortured and killed the other day?"

"I'm not sure there is anything like that. There doesn't seem to be a run on killing ultra-Orthodox Jewish guys. But I can't shake the feeling that something weird is going on with this one. The father-in-law's initial reaction and the follow-up later were just strange. The guy doesn't seem to care about the death in the least. In fact, he seemed relieved. As you know, I don't know that much about ultra-Orthodox, but it's just extraordinary."

Sam said, "The ultra-Orthodox are certainly a bit unusual, but I agree that it sounds like his reaction is slightly off. Why don't you return to the rabbi you found and ask him about it?"

"I could, but I doubt he will tell me that the guy was killed over getting a divorce. Plus, it may not be anything at all about the divorces."

"So, what do you think I can do to help you?"

"Know anyone in organized crime that focuses on the Russian Mob? I've worked with the Italian Mob in Philly but haven't interacted with the Russian group."

"I know a guy: Lawrence Charles. He made it to detective very quickly. Did some time in the special victims unit but then got moved to organized crime. I'm sure he's spent some time with the Italians, but he's probably had some cases cross over into the Russians. I'll call him and see if he can give you some insight. He's a good guy, and I'm sure if he's got any helpful information, he will pass it along."

"Sam, that would be great. I feel I am making something out of nothing with this death sentence over getting a divorce, but I think it's worth a little look."

"I'll give Larry a call. Good luck with finding out anything. Also, I gotta say that this one is even weirder than what you usually come up with. You do come up with some interesting ideas, Sharon."

"That I do, Sam. That I do."

Sharon started looking through some more of her documents. Nothing was jumping out to help her, but then her phone rang. "Detective Levin."

"Sharon, it's Sam. I checked in with Larry, and he might have some insight into the Russian mob, but he is now buried with two cases. He thought he might be able to break loose in a couple of days."

"Sam, that would be great if he can. But who knows, maybe we can have a breakthrough in the next couple of days."

"Hope springs eternal, doesn't it?"

"About the only way, we can keep any sort of positive attitude in what we do for a living. Thanks for getting back to me, Sam."

After she hung up, Sharon leaned back in her chair. She tried to think of some more ideas to try on this case, but it seemed to be loose ends all around. After pondering for a few minutes, she decided what the hell and called the rabbi.

He picked up quickly, "Rabbi Shulman."

"Rabbi Shulman. This is Detective Sharon Levin from yesterday. I was wondering if I could follow up some from our discussion yesterday?"

"Detective, I only have a few minutes, and I don't think I can add more, but go ahead and ask."

"Rabbi, what I'm going to ask about is a bit weird, even by my standards. I wonder if you have ever heard of ultra-Orthodox men being threatened regarding granting a get?"

Shulman raised his voice and said, "Detective, while I have tried to be helpful in your investigation, I think you have now stepped outside the bounds of decency. Are you accusing Jewish men of being threatened and beaten over granting a divorce? If so, I think I will just hang up the phone right now."

Sharon lowered her head even though she was only on the phone. "I apologize, Rabbi, but this case has been strange in several ways. I'm trying to gather as many facts as possible to piece together a possible scenario."

"Well, the only thing I can say to you is that the fact is that Jewish men are not threatened regarding divorces. Yes, there have been a few stories along those lines, but almost all of those crazy ideas have been debunked. We take our religion very seriously, but we're not going to harm someone over a divorce physically. Is that clear?"

"Yes, Rabbi. That is very clear. Again, appreciate all the assistance you have provided. Have a good day."

As Sharon hung up the phone, she couldn't help but think that the rabbi's response was too much. Sure, he was going to defend his faith, but he must have heard some New York and Israeli stories.

Doth the rabbi doth protest too much?

# Chapter Twenty-Two

After my meeting with Arnold Brownstein, I headed off to my evening intermediate accounting class. I had decided to take the subway since my class would be over at about 7:30, and the light would still be up. I had chosen a long time ago not to take the train at night. It would probably be fine, but Sharon had been clear that she didn't want me to take the train at night. And arguing with a Philly detective over security was one I was likely going to lose.

While waiting for the subway train to come, I had the strangest thoughts about family. Somehow with all the discussion about the ultra-Orthodox Jewish community and the role that family plays in that community, I thought about my upbringing in North Carolina. This was not something I pondered very often, but for some strange reason, it was on my mind right now.

So, I was thinking about growing up in a small town in NC called High Point. About 65,000 people. In the middle of the state. I was the only kid that my parents had. My dad was a banker at a local bank, and my mom was a junior-high teacher. Both had attended UNC as the only members of my family who attended college.

I always thought that I was doing okay in school. Wasn't at the top of the class but pretty well ranked. I decided to break out of the family mode and applied to schools other than Carolina. I finally decided on Wake Forest. It was much more expensive than Carolina, but my parents supported me financially as their only child.

I started in the sciences but soon found that I wasn't much of a scientist. I was doing alright in classes but didn't enjoy them, so I switched to economics. Found my stride there.

Once I graduated from Wake, I decided I wanted to get an MBA. I had thought about just getting a job, but I also felt that I should go ahead and knock out the MBA since I was already in school and study mode. But the big thing was that I decided to move away from NC. My parents and friends weren't thrilled but could understand it. I thought about schools in Florida and California but decided that DC was my kind of town. I applied to Georgetown, GW, and American U. I didn't get into Georgetown but got into GW and AU. I liked both schools, but AU looked the most like Wake, with trees, plants, and a quad. I decided on AU.

AU ended up being great after I switched from econ to accounting. I graduated first in my MBA class and got an excellent job with a local accounting firm. But, while I enjoyed studying accounting, I found very quickly that I didn't enjoy doing accounting. After two years in public accounting and completing my CPA requirements, I changed from doing to teaching and applied to UNC's Ph.D. program. I didn't think I would get in, but I did.

I spent almost four years completing my Ph.D. in an accounting degree. When it was time to look for a job, as always with academic careers, I had to do the nationwide search deal. I got a few decent offers, but while interviewing at Temple, I decided that I liked Philly and accepted the job offer Temple.

During my first few years at Temple, I was on the publish or perish plan. I had to ground out the research projects. I liked the teaching, but I sometimes had to shortchange the students because of the tenure research requirements. During my six-year tenure track, I pumped out seven decent articles. Not the top tier, but full enough. I was granted tenure, which was a significant accomplishment for me, and I took the one-semester sabbatical to which I was entitled. I took the opportunity to look at Fulbrights and found that Malta was an exciting place. I applied to the Fulbright in Malta and got it. I did a little teaching and research, but I mostly enjoyed the time away from Temple and the research grind.

While I was strolling down memory lane about my life, a peculiar thing to be doing, the orange line subway came into the City Hall stop so I could head up to Temple. The car wasn't that crowded yet, so there was plenty of space to spread out. But it didn't matter since my stop at Temple was only a few stops on Broad Street.

While I was waiting for my stop at Temple, for some unknown reason, I started to do a bit of a debrief of Sharon's life. I had no idea why I was doing this life analysis for the two of us, but I only had a few minutes, so if I was going to have to our problems quickly, I better get started.

Sharon was born in Philly. Her dad was a cop. He was one of the first Jewish cops in the Northeast part of Philly, so his life as a cop wasn't easy. There was still plenty of antisemitism in the area, and he had to endure a lot of abuse. It wasn't like the movie Serpico, but it wasn't easy.

Sharon came from a big family with four kids, and she was the oldest, so her mom stayed at home. Sharon's family wasn't very religious, but her parents wanted her to get the best education possible. So, they sent their kids to a Jewish parochial school for high school. It was pretty expensive, but her parents worked hard to spring for the private school. This particular school had a decent sports program, and Sharon was a good athlete.

Sharon was very skilled at softball, and she was recruited for some Division 3 college softball programs. The problem was that D3 doesn't provide scholarships, and her family couldn't afford the tuition after providing for a private high school. Sharon thought about taking out loans, but a bit of soul searching led her to decide to follow in her dad's footsteps and become a cop. She took the police exam and did well but didn't get accepted on her first try. However, she was accepted to the police academy the second time and graduated first in her class.

She progressed quickly in the department, mostly because she was good at her job and partially because the department was trying to advance more women. She made detective in only seven years, a very fast track. Her family, particularly her dad, were very proud of her accomplishments.

I was almost at my stop, so I had to hustle about how Sharon and I had met. She was working in robbery at the time, and she had a case where some documents were stolen from a big-time law firm. Sharon and the CSI team found some documents at the law firm. The CSI team examined the records and decided that there might be some white-collar crime, but they weren't sure what it might mean. That's where I came in.

Sharon decided to forego the FBI to do the analysis, and she trolled the internet looking for accounting professors in the area who might be able to do some digging. She made a few phone calls, and all the accounting professors seemed too busy or not interested. However, she gave me a call, and I decided it might be some fun. She gave me all the documents, and after some searching, I found a link between the documents and was able to piece together a plausible way of what was happening. It gave Sharon and the robbery team enough to go on to solve the case.

Neither Sharon nor I thought that we would see each other again, but I decided that I found her fascinating, so I gave her a call. I was very nervous about calling, but I took the plunge. I invited her to The Victor Café, and she accepted. We had a great meal and some fantastic opera. I wasn't sure if we had anything going on as a couple, but I invited her to a concert at the Wells Fargo, and not long later, we cemented ourselves as a couple. Been at it now for almost seven years.

As I pulled into my stop, I had no idea why I was doing this debrief of our lives. Oh well, so much for pondering the imponderables. Time to return to intermediate accounting!

# Chapter Twenty-Three

Isak finally came up with the $25,000 down payment to pay the mob. He had saved enough from his meat cutter job that he had kept squirreled away from his wife. He still wasn't sure how he would get the balance paid, but after finding out about Kaplan's betrayal, he knew he could not let his son-in-law off the hook. The cheating bastard had to pay. In fact, Isak was, in some ways hoping that David would be a hard case for the mob guys to crack. He wanted David to suffer. Didn't want him to die, but Isak believed some motivational pain would be justified in this case.

Isak had delivered the money to Kaplan and gave him his house number where David lived. He also provided a picture of David so they knew what their target looked like. Isak did say to Kaplan that he didn't want his son-in-law killed, but if David resisted signing the get, Isak encouraged Kaplan to persuade David to sign.

Kaplan decided to use Grinburg and Moskowitz again since they had done an excellent job the first time, even though the target was killed. Kaplan told Grinburg and Moskowitz not to kill the guy but to ensure he signed the document.

Grinburg and Moskowitz chose to use the same factory over on Rising Sun. The cops had inspected the place the first time, but Grinburg and Moskowitz had been back, and the place was all quiet again. They decided why to bother finding a new location. This factory was perfect and very convenient for their purpose.

Isak told them that David didn't go out that much since he was a deadbeat and didn't work. He said the only time David goes out is that he sometimes goes over to Petrovsky Market on Bustleton

Avenue, and he usually stops in midafternoon on Tuesdays and Thursdays. Grinburg and Moskowitz decided to hang around the store on Tuesday, waiting for their target.

They waited outside the store the following Tuesday for their mark to arrive. At about 2:45 pm, they saw their target go into the store. They waited until David had done his shopping and was headed to the car. Just as he reached the car, Grinburg grabbed David by his collar while Moskowitz opened the car door, and Grinburg shoved him in. David tried to scream, but Moskowitz already had the chloroform at the ready, and he covered David's nose and quickly was unconscious.

Grinburg and Moskowitz put David in the back seat and headed to the factory. Even though it was daylight, the area was still quiet and empty, just like the first time. They carried David into the factory and tied him up to a metal chair. They put a mask over his mouth so no one would hear him scream. Then they just waited until David woke up. They decided just to play some gin rummy to kill time. Since they were okay with playing cards, it was clear that they were very comfortable with what might come next.

It took about 45 minutes before David woke up. He was still groggy but instantly knew he was tied up and covered his mouth. He started to squirm and grunt through the mask.

Grinburg smiled at David and shook his head. "Don't waste your time wiggling around. We've got you tied up very tight. And obviously, you're wasting your effort trying to scream. We'll have you home by dinner if you do what we ask. I'll let my associate here to explain what is going on."

Moskowitz said, "As my friend said, we have something we need you to do. It's pretty simple. We have a document that you need to sign. It says that you are willing to agree that your wife will be given a Jewish divorce. Simple thing. Just sign it, and we'll all be on our way."

David looked at Grinburg and Moskowitz and shook his head. In fact, he shook his head very hard to show that he was not willing to sign the document.

Grinburg leaned forward and said, "See, we thought you were likely to resist our request. You must understand that there is a hard or easy way to do this. But you need to understand that this will get done, one way or another. And just to illustrate how serious we are, I will tell you that we are the ones who killed Lev Brodsky. I'm sure you don't want to subject yourself to what Lev endured, so make it easy on yourself and just sign. We have a document, and I have a pen. Sign it, and all will be great."

David again shook his head. He nodded his head to indicate that he wanted to say something. Moskowitz said, "I'll remove the gag, but if you decide to scream, we will tie you back up, and you can suffer as the other guy did." He removed David's gag.

David said in a hoarse voice, "Even if I sign that thing, it would never hold up in the Jewish community. Everyone will know I did it under duress and will be invalid."

"Yeah, we thought of that," said Grinburg. "That's why you're going to sign the thing and then tell your father-in-law, wife, and rabbi that you want the divorce. You will make this a public announcement, making it stick."

David looked down and said, "I know that you two can hurt me, even torture me, but I am not going to let my bastard of a father-in-law get away with cutting me out of his money."

Moskowitz smiled. He reached into a pouch that he had and pulled out a taser. He pulled the gag back up on David. He said, "How about we test how things go if you don't do what we ask." Moskowitz started the taser and leaned it over to David's groin. He turned it on, and David screamed so loudly that even through the mask, the mobsters could hear it.

Grinburg said, "Now that is just a little of what is in store for you. We can do this for a long time. The taser battery lasts for a while. Your call, but I strongly encourage you to do what we ask."

Moskowitz added, "Oh, and just if you think that signing the thing and then calling the cops, I will say that that is a terrible idea. You have the two of us who will make your life miserable, but we have friends who will add to your misery. Sign the thing and get this over with. Apparently, you don't love your wife anyway, so move on. It's true you may have to get a job since you will be off the gravy train of the father-in-law, but that's better than having your balls roasted to a crisp which is exactly what we will do."

David looked into their eyes and could tell that these guys weren't kidding. He could tell these guys meant it as much as he wanted to resist. He decided to play along and find a way out of this. He nodded his head.

Grinburg released David's hands so he could sign. He handed the pen, and David signed his name. He gave it back to Grinburg. Grinburg checked to ensure it was correctly signed, and then he tied David back to the chair.

Grinburg said to David, "We're going to take you back to the store. We're not going to knock you out again because I think you know what will happen if you try to escape or scream. It won't end well. Also, I will remind you that if you involve the cops or any other law enforcement group, our associates or we will come back, and the little nudge of the taser before will be only a small taste of what will happen. And you don't want to test us on this. We can keep you alive and in great pain for a long time. We are good at this, so don't do anything stupid."

David nodded. He didn't know how he would get out of this, or even if he could, but he knew that he didn't need any more reminders of how the taser felt. He would play along and then figure out what was next to be done.

The only thing he could hope for was that his father-in-law, Isak, finally grew a pair and didn't want David to be harmed. But David knew that wasn't likely, so he had to do this alone.

# Chapter Twenty-Four

David was dropped off at the store by Grinburg and Moskowitz. Again, they reminded him to keep his mouth shut and that his health will remain good. Things will not be so kind if he says something about what happened at the factory.

When David returned home, he saw that Raisa and Isak were home. He decided he might as well get this over with. He didn't know what his next steps were going to be, but he was afraid that if he didn't follow the mobsters' instructions, he was sure he would be badly harmed.

He entered the house where Raisa and Isak were talking in the kitchen. He said, "Hi. I need to talk to you both for a few minutes. Please sit at the table, and I'll tell you what's happening."

Isak actually sort of smiled because he had a good idea of what was going to be the topic. David said, "So, as both know, I haven't been working for a while. I don't feel guilty about that, but I've made a big decision since I've had time to think. I want a divorce from Raisa."

Raisa said, "What do you mean you want a divorce? I know we've had some troubles, but where does this notion of a divorce come out of nowhere?"

"I've just given it some thought. Lately, I'm just not happy right now. I know that by divorcing you, Isak will no longer support me financially, but I've decided that I'm not satisfied with our marriage. I want a divorce."

While Raisa started to cry, Isak tried to hide his smirk. Obviously, the mobsters had been successful in getting David to sign. Isak was somewhat disappointed that David wasn't bleeding or in apparent pain, but Isak was pretty sure that David wasn't the type to just go with what the mobsters wanted without some encouragement. He thought with great pride that David deserved it.

Isak said, "Well, I'm sorry you feel that way. However, if you feel strongly about this, then we should go ahead and dissolve the marriage. You know that we need to obtain a get."

David reached into his pocket and pulled out the signed paper. He said, "I already have the document, and we can do it quickly. I see no reason to waste any time. Let's just get it done."

Raisa was still crying, so Isak took the paper. He said, "Well, we first need to notify Rabbi Shulman that you've signed the get. That will cover the Jewish law, and then we can contact a lawyer about the legal side of making it happen."

Finally, Raisa said through tears, "I can't believe you two are being so calm about this. We have been married for many years and have children. Both of you make it sound like we're going on a trip to the grocery. This is our marriage and family we're talking about. This is a huge deal, and you two seem to believe the marriage is over, and we all move on. Dad, how can you be casual about this?"

Isak replied, "Raisa, I think David sounds like he's already made his decision. I don't see any reason to protract the inevitable. Let's just get this over with and move on. You can find other marriage possibilities, so I don't see why you should stretch it out. Just get it done with."

"I agree with Isak," said David. "I've made up my mind, and I would say that having already provided a get shows how serious I am. I will find a cheap hotel to stay at starting tonight. Raisa, if you don't contest this, I'm sure we can make this happen in a hurry. Since I have already provided the get and met the Jewish requirements, the other legal matters should be pretty simple."

Raisa screamed at both of them. "I still can't believe you are both so laissez-faire about this thing. I'm going upstairs to talk to my mother. Maybe she cares about what happens to my marriage and children. Clearly, the two of you don't." With that, Raisa stormed out of the kitchen.

David leaned close to Isak and said, "I know you had something to do with forcing me to do this. I just want to promise you that we're not done. You may have won this round, but the game is not over."

Isak smiled and said, "That's what happens when you cheat on my daughter. And you can threaten me all you want to, but, in the end, I'm paying these mobsters a good bit of money, so I'm pretty sure I will win. By the way, you don't have to answer this, but did you have an affair?"

"You bet I did! I needed to have sex with a beautiful woman, and Raisa is not that one."

"Then I hope she was worth it because now you'll need to get a job—bad break for you. Also, I was hoping you could call Rabbi Shulman and tell him about the big change. He's the first one in the community that needs to know."

David replied, "And why should I do anything else you ask me to do?"

"Because, as I said, I'm in charge, and you need to follow my instructions. Call him right now and make it happen." With that, Isak left the kitchen and headed out to his car.

David was furious about Isak's attitude, but he also knew that for now, Isak was in charge. But he was going to ensure that Isak didn't stay in control. Of that, he was pretty sure.

David called the synagogue and asked for Rabbi Shulman. By chance, the rabbi was available, and David's call was patched over to

Shulman. Rabbi Shulman said, "David, I'm surprised to hear from you. You have been keeping a pretty low profile of late. How are you doing?"

"Rabbi, I'm doing fine, but I have some news you need to hear. Raisa and I are getting a divorce. I've already signed a get, so I'm sure it will happen."

Shulman said, "I'm very sorry to hear that. Can I have a meeting with you and Raisa and see if there is anything I can do or say that can keep you two together? You've been together for a long time, and you have kids. You know that our community frowns on divorce. Surely we can find a way that you can keep your marriage together."

"Sorry, Rabbi, but my mind is made up. We have hit the infamous irreconcilable differences, so it's time to end this marriage. I am only telling you because our Jewish laws require that you be informed. In fact, I don't need to talk about it or get any advice. I think we will move fairly quickly to make this happen."

Shulman said, "Well, it certainly sounds like you have made a decision, but I would suggest caution in that it sounds like you're moving too quickly. Why are you in such a hurry?"

"Doesn't matter, but that's the way it is. Also, I have a lot of things to take care of right now, so I will have to hang up. Have a good day, Rabbi."

Shulman hung up his phone. His first thought was that there were now two gets in play with his community. He knew that such a thing was improbable, possible, but unlikely, so he felt he had to do something to find out what was happening.

He recalled the name of the detective who had investigated Lev's murder. He made a couple of calls to the police and finally got the phone number of the detective he had met. He called the number, and after three rings, he heard, "Detective Levin."

"Detective Levin, this is Rabbi Shulman. We spoke not long ago. There has been another question raised regarding Jewish gets, and I would like to talk to you about what has recently transpired. Any chance you might have some time today to talk to me?"

"Rabbi, I will make some time. I can come over around 3 pm. Does that work?"

"That would be fine. I look forward to seeing you."

Sharon couldn't help but wonder what had happened when she hung up. Why would Shulman call her? Indeed, he knew more about Jewish divorces than she did. Then it hit her! Shulman must think that someone else has been coerced into a Jewish divorce.

Maybe now she could finally make some serious progress on this case.

# Chapter Twenty-Five

At 3 pm, Sharon arrived at the shul on Castor Avenue. She knocked on the door, and a woman opened it. Sharon said that she had an appointment with Rabbi Shulman. She told Sharon to take a seat while she checked on the rabbi. After a few minutes, she directed Sharon where to go.

Sharon walked into the same room she went to the first time. Rabbi Shulman said, "Detective, please come in. As before, can I get you some water?"

"No, Rabbi. I'm fine. What's going on?"

"Well, Detective, what has happened is that another member of our synagogue has decided to get a divorce. He called me this morning to tell me he has already signed the get and wants this divorce to proceed quickly."

Sharon replied, "And I guess that struck you as unusual."

"As I mentioned, we have divorces in our small community, but it is quite uncommon for the male to be in such a hurry to sign the get. In fact, sometimes, the male negotiates for something that almost seems like a severance package. This does not appear to be the case in this instance."

"What's the guy's name? Also, what does he do for a living?"

Shulman said, "His name is David Katz. At present, my understanding is that he is unemployed. He has apparently been unemployed for a good while."

"Isn't that strange? Don't ultra-Orthodox men strongly need to provide for their family?"

"That's quite true, and David is certainly an outlier. Apparently, he had decided that his father-in-law, Isak Zylberman, should provide for him and the rest of his family."

"I am going to assume that would not be the norm?"

"It would not be, but it does occasionally happen. This haste in getting a divorce is more unusual, particularly since David relied on Isak for support."

Sharon inquired, "So what do you think happened here?"

Shulman hesitated for a moment and then said in a calm voice, "Maybe I was wrong about Jewish men being forced into divorces."

"That's where I was heading, but I am shocked that you are admitting that it might have happened."

"Detective Levin, you need to understand that a big part of my job is maintaining how pure my shul operates. I have to adhere to strict guidelines prescribed by ultra-Orthodox leaders. I must be cautious of how I approach any controversy within my shul. Without any substantial evidence that wrongdoing had transpired, I had to err on the side of caution, which I did."

"But now you think something is unorthodox religiously and perhaps illegal is happening.

"That is exactly what I'm thinking right now. How should we proceed?"

"Let me huddle with a couple of associates at the station, and I will get back to you as soon as possible. And thank you for coming forward and talking to me. I'm sure it wasn't easy to make that call."

"It surely was not, but I must consider the sanctity of my synagogue and its members. If there are irreligious or illegal activities, then I am required by Jewish law to take steps to correct them."

"Good for you, Rabbi," said Sharon. "As I said, I'll get in touch as soon as possible."

While Sharon was headed back to the precinct, Arnold Brownstein was getting ready to have a complicated conversation. He knew the Russian mob would not be happy that someone was looking over their books, but he had to tell them something.

He knew the phone number for Mikhail Rabinovich, and after much hesitation, he made the call. Rabinovich picked up on the second ring thanks to caller id. He said, "Yes, Mr. Accountant. What can I do for you?"

"Mikhail, please don't get too upset, but I have a bit of bad news."

"As you know, Arnold, I don't like bad news. What is the problem?"

"An accounting professor at Temple University is looking into the books for Petrovsky Markets."

Rabinovich said, "And why would an accounting professor at Temple be looking into the books at Petrovsky? It's just a few small food markets. Yeah, we funnel some cash through them, but it's a pretty small amount compared to what we launder. I know you do their books, and I assume you keep our books very tidy, so what's the problem."

Brownstein replied, "Okay, as you know, we have been moving a lot of cash in and out of the Petrovsky operation, but that should be fine. We know how to move the cash in a hushed manner. And you know that we decided to move some cash into that little startup, TechSounds, to shelter additional money from taxes. We've been using a lot of cryptocurrencies for that company. The problem is that the two kids who started the company and that investor we know, John Flannigan, decided to set up TechSounds as a public company for tax purposes. It made sense at the time, but now something has come up. There is an oversight organization called the Public Company Accounting Oversight Board. Once this professor started looking into TechSounds, that opened the door to Petrovsky. He has access through the Financial Crimes Enforcement Network to track some of the cash flowing around in and out of both Petrovsky and TechSounds."

"And what does all this mean?" asked Mikhail.

"What it means is that the Financial Crimes Enforcement Network has some authority to pour over your books, and if they find something amiss, they can contact the FBI to begin legal proceedings against us. It could become a big problem."

Mikhail said, "Arnold, I must say that I am very disappointed that this has happened. We pay you well, both over and under the table, to make sure this type of issue doesn't become a problem. You have made an accounting problem my problem; that's not how this is supposed to work."

"I understand, but we still need to do something about his."

Mikhail chuckled and said, "And what's the name of this nosy accounting professor's name?"

"His name is Ben Stone, and as I told you, he is a professor at Temple."

"Arnold, I will take care of this for you, but you need to know that I don't do favors for free. You'll have to figure out how to compensate me in some fashion for doing this. Give it some thought." With that, Rabinovitch hung up the phone.

Brownstein also hung up his phone, but he sat for just a minute. He knew that whatever "compensation" Rabinovich had in mind would probably not be cheap and likely fun. The only thing he took as a form of consolation was that good professor Stone was perhaps going to have even less fun than Brownstein was going to have.

# Chapter Twenty-Six

Sharon decided to bring her Jewish expert, Sam Bernstein, back into her office. She had called Sam, and he came into Sharon's office.

Sam said, "So you need some more Jewish education?"

"Actually, no. Rabbi Shulman called me and told me that another congregation member had signed a get to get divorced. The fellow, David Katz, just called him on the phone to tell the rabbi that he was getting a divorce and had already signed the get. Shulman was surprised that another issue with a get had popped up again with his shul. He has now changed his mind that there maybe be something going on with men being forced into signing the divorce papers. But he doesn't know what to do next, and to be honest, I'm not sure either. I seriously doubt that this guy Katz will say anything other than he decided to divorce his wife, which is not illegal. Anyway, got any ideas on what to do?"

Sam said, "Funny you should ask. Because of all this happening in the Jewish community, I decided to delve into the story                                                                                    of The Prodfather you told me about. It ended up being that the FBI had to stage a sting operation to get those guys. Maybe that's the way to go."

"But I need someone to be the target of the sting operation, and I don't have anyone to do that."

"You do now, and you're talking to him."

Sharon said, "You're willing to go undercover to try setting up this sting?"

"Sure, why not? Sharon, I know you well and trust you to ensure I'm not harmed, so sign me up. If these fathers-in-law are paying to have their sons-in-law under duress sign these papers, that is a huge insult to Judaism, even to someone like me who isn't that religious. Yeah, I'm willing to be the target if need be."

"Well, Sam, that is being a pretty standup guy willing to take such a risk. But, yeah, I will make sure you are kept safe and sound."

Sam asked, "So what do you think you need to do next?"

"Well, Ben and I met some FBI folks when we were down at the Outer Banks of North Carolina. I know Ben has been in touch with one of them, and she offered some help on Ben's case about possible money laundering. I'll reach out to see if she has time to get involved with this sting operation. I know that the FBI does many of those things, and she may have insight that we don't have."

"That sounds like a plan, Sharon. Once you've got the basic layout, bring me in, and we'll make it happen. As I said, this whole thing is a bit personal to me, so I'm all in."

"I'll reach out to Emily at the FBI, and if she wants to get involved and has time to do so, I'll start putting the plan in place. And yes, once we have a rudimentary idea, I'll bring you in, and we'll set it up."

Sam said, "Go for it, Sharon. Let's bring in these idiot Jewish dads willing to do anything to get their daughters a divorce. This sickens me."

After Sam left her office, Sharon decided she needed to sit back and figure out her next steps. She got herself a coffee refill, closed the door to her office, and sat back to ponder some. She'd been involved with a lot of nutty stuff over the years, Malta, Finland, and even the Outer Banks, but this was a new one for her!

While Sharon was doing some pondering in her office, Rabinovich had called Grinburg and Moskowitz into his office. When they arrived, they took a seat across from Rabinovich's chair. He said, "So gentlemen, we have another issue other than getting paid for the second get we got signed. Apparently, we have a nosey accounting professor who is looking into our financial books. Our

CPA partner said the guy has already dug up some possible issues, but there may be more, so we need to stop this now."

Moskowitz said, "What do you want us to do, boss? Just scare him off for the time being?"

"If that will suffice, then we can just stop there. But if that doesn't work, we may have to be a little more forceful."

Grinburg and Moskowitz both nodded. They both knew what that meant. Grinburg said, "So where do we find this guy, boss?"

"We know he works at Temple, but that is probably too obvious. Too many people around. Our accountant friend did a little digging and discovered that this professor lives downtown near Rittenhouse Square. I have the exact address. I think you two should go to his home and discuss Petrovsky Markets, and how it would be in his best interest to stay away from it. He's a bean counter and a professor, so I don't think you need to worry about him causing much trouble. Just put a little fear into his thinking, and I'm sure he will back off."

Grinburg asked, "Given how we have been handling these Jewish guys, how far should we go with this guy?"

Rabinovich smiled and said, "I don't think you need to kidnap him and take him to the factory. And you shouldn't carry a taser under your jacket. He's a goofy accounting guy, so like I said, scare him a little, and that will be enough."

Moskowitz asked, "When should we do it?"

"Might as well get it out of the way. Take care of it tonight."

Grinburg and Moskowitz nodded again to Rabinovich. They figured this would be an easy, even more straightforward task than the two times we had to break out the taser. They thought being an accounting teacher would be about as easy a job as possible.

They didn't know that the accounting professor's girlfriend is a Philadelphia homicide detective who always carries her service revolver. But they were going to find out soon enough!

# Chapter Twenty-Seven

I was down at my office doing some grading for my intermediate class. I was behind on my grading because I had been spending a lot of time on my effort to find what Petrovsky Markets and TechSounds were doing. I had a decent idea but needed to be ready because I have a meeting in three days down at Brownstein and Williams. But, even back as an undergrad, I was not too fond of it when professors didn't return exams in a timely fashion. I had one guy down at UNC who rarely returned an exam before the next one was due. Not knowing where I stood grade-wise was very aggravating, so I tried not to do that since I was on the other side of that issue.

My phone rang, and I said, "Dr. Stone."

"Well, I have some interesting news, Dr. Stone," said Sharon.

"Does it have anything to do with food or sex because those are my primary issues right now?"

"Bad break for you because it's not about those things. But I found out there is another ultra-Orthodox guy from the same synagogue as the guy who was killed and has decided to sign a get."

I inquired, "How did you find out about that?"

"That's what's strange. The same rabbi whom I talked to about Jewish gets and the like called me about this new edition. He said that while it is not unprecedented, it's strange to have such events happen so quickly together. But, more importantly, he admitted that maybe something is amiss and that there might be someone who is forcing these guys to sign these gets."

"So maybe Tony Soprano is in the business of forcing guys to sign the forms."

"Something like that, but I doubt the culprit is Italian. I'm leaning towards the Russians, but I don't have that nailed down yet. But I am certainly making some progress. I spoke to Sam Bernstein, and we're trying to set up a sting operation. I have a call into Emily Keen with the FBI to see if she and the agency want to get involved. I know she helped you get assistance from the Financial Crimes Enforcement Network, so I also decided to reach out to her on this issue."

"She's great, and I'm sure she is willing to help if her schedule works. But more importantly, I feel that dinner will be late tonight, if ever."

Sharon snickered and said, "I don't plan on pulling an all-nighter, but it might be a little late. Say 8 pm. Does that work for you?"

"I'll get some snacks over at one of the food trucks to tide me over. What do you want for our late dinner?"

"Hit the Mexican one you found. That was great food."

"Consider it done. Let me know if your plans change, but I will shoot for 8."

"Sound great. Love you!"

"Back at you!"

I just got off the phone with Ben when Sharon got a call. "Detective Levin,"

"Sharon, it is Emily Keen from the FBI returning your call."

"Emily, thanks so much for calling me back. I know you helped Ben with his accounting issue, but I've got a new problem. I've been involved with the ultra-Orthodox Jewish community here in Philly. There was an ultra-Orthodox guy who was killed at an abandoned factory. He had been tortured with what looked like a taser. We've been trying to gather information for a while but had a lot of theories, but not much too solid. We were looking into whether or not someone tortured this guy to get him to sign a Jewish divorce decree, what's called a get. I've had a couple more religious guys from the force help me. I've even been involved with a rabbi. Then today, I just got a call from the same rabbi that another member of his congregation had decided to get a divorce. On the first one, I tried the rabbi on the issue of someone forcing him, but the rabbi was very defensive that such a thing would not happen. Now with this second one, the rabbi is more amenable to discussing such a possibility. More importantly, I spoke to another Philly cop, and we think we might need to set up a sting operation to find out what is happening. The rabbi said that he would help in any way that he could. Just wondering what you think?"

Emily chuckled and said, "Okay, I have heard that you and sometimes Ben get the strangest cases, but this is pretty way out there. Someone is physically threatening a Jewish guy to get him to give his wife a divorce. That is out there, Sharon."

"I know. I guess I should call you occasionally with a "normal" case, so you know I sometimes have one. But yeah, you only hear about the weird ones. Anyway, do you have any time that you could come down to Philly and give us a hand? A sting operation is not in my wheelhouse, and I could use some FBI insight."

Emily said, "Let me talk to my boss. I've got a couple of cases, but they are not pressing. Let me try to get in touch with you tomorrow. I'm sure he's buried in meetings today, so I'll try to catch him at the end of the day."

"Emily, that would be great. I really would help any insight you might have as to how to play this."

"I'll be in touch, Sharon," and Emily hung up.

Sharon felt that if Emily could be approved to assist, that would be a big help in this crazy thing. She knew from experience that the nuttier your case is, the more people she knew she had to bring to bear on it. She didn't like the cliché "Thinking outside the box," but between Malta, Belgium, Finland, New Orleans, and the Outer Banks, she knew that the usual tried and true investigative approach probably wouldn't get it done on her own. More investigators can come up with more ideas.

Because of being a cop, Sharon usually figured that her case, versus anything Ben the accounting prof was doing, was more likely to involve some danger. Little did she know that Ben's case was the one that would put them in immediate peril!

# Chapter Twenty-Eight

I finished a lot of my grading, which made me feel good because I have been slacking off some on my actual accounting job for the first time in a while. I have been mainly teaching the same classes for years, so I can fall out of bed and do them. And also, no one has been showing up for office hours with questions. I didn't know if I was doing such an excellent job teaching that they didn't need my help or if they somehow figured out a way to cheat. I knew that almost every previous exam was available online, so I had to write a new one for every test. Back in the day, I could use the test banks for my exams, but those days were long gone. It's true that even when I was at Wake Forest, the fraternities tried to keep old exams if they could get ahold of them, but now it is just too easy. Added to my workload, some to make new exams all the time, but it's just how academia is these days.

I took the subway down to City Hall and walked the short distance to my house. I went in and decided I had already done enough Temple work for the day, so I moved on to PCAOB work and looked into Petrovsky and Techsounds. I reviewed all my files on the matter and laid out everything, so I was ready for my meeting with the audit partner.

It was coming up at 7 pm, so I decided to check in with Sharon to see when she would likely get home. I gave her a call, and she answered on the first ring. "I'm guessing this is Dr. Stone."

"Yes, it is. Since you used my name, is it already so late that someone might call you on your case?"

She said, "Place is pretty dead right now. I'm packing up, and I should still be home by 8. You should go ahead and put for

Mexican. I should be there before the food arrives, assuming you're having it delivered."

"Mexican food delivered on Door Dash is on its way."

"See you very soon."

I ordered the food and asked for delivery. They told me that it should be there in about a half-hour. That would likely do just fine for Sharon's arrival.

About 20 minutes later, my doorbell rang. I thought Door Dash was just a little early, so I opened the door. Two heavyset guys were standing in the doorway. One of them said in a heavy accent, "Are you the accounting guy from Temple?"

"If you mean Doctor Stone, then yes, I am he. What can I do for you?"

The first guy said, "We represent someone regarding Petrovsky Markets. My friend and I are here to encourage you to leave Petrovsky alone. Stay away from looking at our books."

"What is Petrovsky Markets? I have no idea what you're talking about."

The slightly bigger guy said, "It is not a good idea to screw us around. We know you have been looking into Petrovsky's books, and we want you to stop.

For some reason, I decided I didn't feel like being pushed around right now, and I replied, "Assuming I am involved in looking at their books, why would I want to stop that? I am doing my job and certainly not doing anything inappropriate."

The second guy said, "I don't think you understand. My friend used the word encourage, but I would be more likely to say demand."

This is the second time I have had someone show up at my door to threaten me to stop doing my job. The first time was with the Langritz problem, and the local mod was involved with that one. I definitely had the same feeling that these guys had mob connections, but the heavy accents said they weren't local. I also knew Sharon was not far from home, so I decided to stall a little till she got there.

"Gentlemen, I don't understand why this is happening. I'm doing some accounting work, and you two are here threatening me. What the hell is going on here?"

The second guy said, "It doesn't matter why we are doing this. All that matters is that we are very serious that you need to back off on Petrovsky. Otherwise, you might find yourself in some serious physical trouble."

I knew that was coming, but I was surprised by how overt they were. And how quickly they had upped the threat quotient. I knew the most straightforward way was to say that I would do what they said. But I also knew I wasn't going to back off, so the best plan I could think of was to continue to delay them until Sharon got there.

I said, "But gentlemen, I am getting paid to do this accounting work. Are you willing to compensate me for walking away from this work?"

Both guys smiled at each other. The first one said, "No, we are not going to pay you to back off. You're going to back off because that will keep you healthy. Do you have any more questions?"

Just as I was about to say something, Sharon said, "Well, the only question I have is whether you want to raise your hands peacefully while I take you into custody, or will I have to wound one of you or the other to make the question clear?"

Both guys turned and saw Sharon's gun pointed right between them. The first guy moved faster than Sharon anticipated, swung his arm around, and knocked her to the ground. Both guys took off quickly. Sharon was up in a flash, but both guys were faster than she thought, and they were around the corner instantly. As she followed them around the same corner, she saw they had already slipped away. She was thinking of chasing after them, but she decided they might come back after Ben, so she needed to stay near him just in case.

Sharon returned to my house and said, "Okay, what the hell was that all about? You didn't tip the Door Dash delivery guy enough?"

"It's great that you can make jokes after I ended up again with someone threatening me at my front door. This time I got two guys rather than one."

"Well, at least neither of these guys reached for a weapon. That's an improvement from the first time."

"Boy, I feel so much safer right now."

# Chapter Twenty-Nine

Right after we went back into my house, the door rang again, but this time it was Door Dash with the Mexican food. I had already tipped through the app and just took the food.

Sharon knew I was still rattled, so she tried to bring me back down a little. She knew her first response was to laugh a little to break the tension, but now she had to be a bit serious.

She said, "Okay, so enough with my jokes. What the hell happened here?"

"I had just placed the order for the Mexican food, and when the door rang, I figured the food just got there a little early. When I opened the door, those two goons were standing there. Yes, they had no weapons drawn, but it was still a little nerve-racking. But I knew you were close by, so I decided the try to stall them until you arrived."

"Pretty brave. Maybe a little stupid, but still brave. I assume they were there to threaten you over something, right?"

"Yes, this time, the issue was Petrovsky Markets. The two guys said I needed to back off from looking at Petrovsky's finances. And yep, they got around to threatening me with bodily harm if I didn't comply."

"They didn't say anything before they ran off, so did you get anything unusual out of them?" said Sharon.

"Thick accent. It sounded like Russian, Ukraine, or even maybe Polish. They didn't say much but took turns speaking, and both had similar accents."

"Get a look at their clothing or the like that might indicate anything useful to know about them?"

"Just had standard fare of jeans, sneakers, and hoodies. Nothing that stood out. The only thing I have is the accent."

Sharon said, "Well, I guess you should take some solace in knowing that you thought Petrovsky was dirty in some way and was right. Two muscle guys showing up to threaten you says something is shady at Petrovsky.

"Yeah, but I thought I just had some shady accounting going on. Now I seemingly have some guys who look and act like mobsters involved in this thing."

"Ben, when you told me about the possibility of money laundering being involved, I knew that someone rougher than a CPA firm was somehow going to be involved. Didn't you?"

"I guess I did sort of think that this could be more complicated than just money. Many of our joint money laundering investigations also bring the mob or the like into the picture. I just hadn't pictured two mob enforcers showing up at my front door again."

"We are going to have to be much more cautious around you than I thought we would need. And I think you need to call Emily with the FBI first thing in the morning. I have her coming down Friday to start trying to set up the sting operation, but now we have this new wrinkle with Petrovsky. I don't know if her boss will let her be involved in two investigations simultaneously, but I think we need to talk to her before she leaves for Philly. I think talking her boss into two investigations simultaneously is a discussion best done in person. Who knows? Maybe our two cases are somehow related. I can't think of how, but you never know these days."

"I will give her a call first thing in the morning. Anyway, do you think there is a chance that those guys might come back tonight?"

"I doubt it. They saw my gun, so I doubt they would come back and test my marksmanship tonight. Why, are you hungry?"

"Sort of lost my appetite, but I could surely use a drink. We've had a number of these issues both here and abroad, but I'm still now as used to them as you are," said Ben.

"Darling, allow me to mix you a delicious cocktail. What would you like?"

"Scotch rocks would be fine. Single malt, please."

"I guess this thing rattled you more than I thought. Don't worry; we're going to have the Philadelphia police, and likely the FBI might even get involved. We're going to keep you safe."

"I'm sure you will. It's just that accounting professors are supposed to have slow and even boring jobs. We just keep running around adding up numbers."

Sharon said, "True, but you would likely get bored without the excitement we have with some of our adventures. Plus, you are performing an essential task with the PCAOB group. You're helping to make sure that investors have solid financial statements with which to make investments. That's a pretty important thing to do. We saw what happened during the financial meltdown of 2008 because the financial numbers were often crap. Almost brought down the entire world's financial system.

"Yeah, but I still want to retire at a ripe age at Temple."

"Not to worry, Ben. We're going to keep you safe and sound. Let me get your drink, and you sit back and relax. I'll set the table for our Mexican feast, and then we will sit back and find something entertaining to watch. We'll take the rest of this night off and pick it up in the morning. Does that sound okay?"

"Maybe the black teddy thing would help me to unwind from all the drama of the day."

Sharon smiled and said, "Nice to know you still have your priorities in place. Yeah, maybe I could break out the teddy."

I thought to myself: I am lucky to have this woman in my life. One of these days, I'm going to have to figure out if we need to take the next step in this relationship. But I'm not going to ponder it right now. It's teddy night!

But while I was excited about teddy night, I didn't know that Sharon's suggestion that our cases were somehow related wasn't as farfetched as it sounded. Who would have thought that ultra-Orthodox Jewish gets, Russian food markets, and a small tech company would somehow align with each other, but as Sharon noted, who knows these days? Crazier shit has happened with some of our adventures!

# Chapter Thirty

We ended up having a fantastic night. The food was great, and the teddy had done its magic. But we woke up early, and both of us quickly decided that today would be tough. Lots of things had to happen.

Sharon headed to the station at 7:30 because she needed to speak to her captain and find out how much support she could expect to keep me safe. She knew that the captain would be sympathetic to my plight, but she also knew what she wanted me to be secure, and that would require some round-the-clock protection which would be expensive. She would really have to call in any favors she had with the captain.

At around 9 am, I decided to put in a call to Emily Keen at the FBI. She picked up on the first ring. "Emily Keen."

"Emily, it's Ben Stone in Philadelphia."

"Ben, it's nice to hear from you. I'm sure you know that I'm headed up to Philly tomorrow to help Sharon with her ultra-Orthodox get investigation. Why are you calling? Something up with her case?"

I replied, "Actually, it's not about her case. Or at least we don't know if it is somehow related to her case. Two tough guys showed up at my house last night and threatened me regarding an accounting case that I'm involved in. Lucky for me, Sharon got to my house right after the two guys showed up, and she was able to scare them off. They ran away very quickly, and she couldn't catch them."

"Wow, I am sorry that happened to you. You two just can't have a simple day, can you?"

"We sometimes do, but not right now. Anyway, Sharon is meeting with her captain to try to get some security for me, and I guess her. But we want to ask you a favor. Since you are already coming up to Philly, do you think you might be able to offer some assistance with my situation? Sharon thought you might be able to offer some ideas of how we might proceed with my side of crazy right now."

"Ben, I am happy to help though I am not sure how much I can do. My boss only released me to help Sharon, so I will not have anyone else backing me up."

"As I said, Sharon will get as much help from the Philly cops as she can. She's in pretty good with the captain. She really just wants to run by some ideas about the new wrinkle."

"Not a problem. When I get there tomorrow, I'll make sure I huddle with you two about your cases. I look forward to working together with you two."

I said, "Thank you a lot, Emily. I also look forward to seeing you again." With that, I hung up.

I decided to have another coffee, sit back, and consider what had happened last night. While I was somewhat nervous the previous night, I'm surprised I decided to keep those bullies around until Sharon arrived. I guess it was the best idea I could come up with on the fly. Like she said, pretty brave but also a little stupid.

I tried hard to ensure I didn't seem too shaken in front of Sharon. She had a lot on her plate, too, so I thought I needed to portray that I was good to go. But even though I knew that Sharon would provide security, and now I had some additional help with Emily Keen, I still felt pretty nervous. Sharon and I had been through many scary situations at home and abroad, but for some reason, this one had me rattled. What I needed to do was to find something to do to occupy my mind for a bit. I knew that the best thing to do was focus on work with Temple or PCAOB, but I just didn't have that in me right now. I thought that I could always watch some TV or do some reading, but even that didn't seem to do the trick. As I was fumbling about what to do, my mind returned to pondering life, work, and Sharon that I had done a while ago on my way to work. I still wasn't sure what prompted this evaluation, but it seemed that I wasn't entirely done with it because it was back on my mind.

I knew that I loved Sharon, and she loved me; that was very clear. We had occasionally discussed whether we should get married. We had even talked about children. The problem was that neither of us felt strongly about either issue to take a serious look at where we were.

I had been an only child, so I wasn't wholly convinced of my desire for children. Some of my extended family members had kids, but that didn't make me feel the burning need to have a kid. Sharon had come up with a good-sized family, but that had in many ways taken her off the hook to have a kid. There were plenty of kids in her family, so she didn't feel she had to further the Levin name as others had already seen to that.

It was actually sort of funny when we had these discussions. We always thought and discussed these issues almost in a hypothetical manner as if we weren't serious. In fact, when we did have such deliberations, we almost always ended up laughing out loud as if the whole thing was a joke. We both knew we were doing that to avoid a serious discussion on the issues.

But for some reason, this time, I found that I was not as big on joking about it. Maybe it was because of all the scary and possibly deadly things that had happened in our lives of late. The Philly mob with Langritz. The Ukrainian mob in Malta. More mob in Belgium. A female serial killer in Finland. A crazy kid who wanted to play the blues. The Dixie Mafia in New Orleans. The Jamaican mob in the Outer Banks. All of this started to make me feel that life can be short and that sometimes today is a better day to do something than waiting for tomorrow.

I decided that once our two cases were wrapped up, Sharon and I needed to have a serious discussion about where we were. I wasn't sure she would be that open to such a discussion, but I knew I needed to try.

I was sure Hoegaarden wouldn't make the grade with this little chat. Maybe time to break out the Dom Perignon!

# Chapter Thirty-One

The three head honchos of the Russian mob, Rabinovich, Reznick, and Kaplan, were extremely angry with Grinburg and Moskowitz. They had summoned the two henchmen to explain what happened and why the two had to run away. Rabinovich was incredibly pissed because he felt it made his whole operation look weak.

Grinburg and Moskowitz knew that they would be racked over the coals by his bosses. The Russian mob takes its position of strength and the ability to be in charge very seriously. Grinburg and Moskowitz knew that the bosses would not be happy that they didn't deliver on what was expected.

Grinburg and Moskowitz got to the office ready for a beating, at least a verbal one, and maybe even knocked around a bit. They came in through the back door in case anyone was watching for them.

When they came into the office, Rabinovich said, "Okay, why don't you two losers take a seat?"

Grinburg and Moskowitz knew this would be bad, but they also knew that coming up with excuses would only make it worse. Russians have no tolerance for justifications, just results. They just took a seat and waited.

Rabinovich said, "So you both know you screwed up, big time. All we wanted you to do is scare a puny little accounting professor into leaving Petrovsky Markets alone. Pretty easy, so I don't understand why it screwed up so much."

Grinburg said, "Sir, we knew exactly what you expected, and we were ready to take care of business. We didn't expect this professor to have a woman with him carrying a gun. She came up behind us, and we were caught off guard. We were probably lucky to get away from her. Moskowitz knocked her over, and we ran away from her. We found a way to run away from her, and we hid behind some garbage cans until we were sure she was gone."

"You hid from a woman! That is pathetic."

"But, sir, we knew that she had a gun. Yes, we were armed, but we didn't think having a shootout in the middle of the Rittenhouse area downtown would be good for business," said Moskowitz.

Kaplan said, "Okay, there is some sense to that. But what about coming back later at night to finish your job?"

Grinburg said, "Since this whole thing went very sideways, we feel we needed to talk to you three before we made another move. We know this screwup was our fault and want to fix it, but we didn't want to decide to check in with you."

Kaplan replied, "You two are trying to cover your asses. But I can't say that I wouldn't be doing the same thing if I had screwed up as much as that. But you're also right that we need to fix this. We cannot have any loose ends like that. Mikhail, what do you think we should do next?"

Mikhail said, "Well, I've already found out who this woman is. I called a couple of cops who do us favors now and then. One of the cops said he knew there was a homicide cop named Sharon Levin, whose boyfriend is some kind of professor. Gotta be the ones involved. How many professors have cops as their girlfriend?"

Kaplan said, "So we know who the woman made us look so weak. And I think we know what we need to do. And we know that both of you dumbasses are to ones to do it. You two need to rough up the professor and the cop. Probably not kill them because killing a cop brings on a lot of heat, but still, let them both know not to mess around with Russians."

Moskowitz asked, "But, sir, she's a cop, and you know that because of our first attempt, she will be on the lookout. She may even have some additional help from other cops. I'm not worried about getting hurt or anything, but what happens if she pulls her gun again?"

Kaplan smiled and grabbed Moskowitz by his collar. He said, "For a guy who says he's not worried about getting hurt, you are taking a big risk. We expect you to carry out our orders, or a bitch cop and an egghead professor will not be your biggest problem. Do you understand?"

"Yes, sir. We understand. When do you want us to make this happen?"

Rabinovich replied, "We want it to happen soon. Tomorrow night would be best. Since we know where the guy lives, we want you to break in around 3 am while they sleep. Just smack them around to teach them that we're serious guys and to stay away from the accounting company that does the books for Petrovsky and the tech company."

Reznick hadn't said anything, but his cell phone rang just then. He decided to take the call. He had a short conversation, and then he turned to the group. "So, I just found out, from a cop I pay, that the bitch cop is involved in investigating the ultra-Orthodox guy we killed and even the one we just scared into signing the paper."

Kaplan said, "That makes it much more complicated."

Rabinovich smiled and said, "Actually, it makes it much simpler. Two birds. We take care of the Jewish angle and the accounting one. But now we have to up the ante. The plan was to scare the cop and the professor, but now we need to end them."

Neither Grinburg nor Moskowitz knew what to say. As Kaplan had already said, it's not good business to kill a cop. The police will bring all their forces to bear on finding the culprit when a cop is involved. Finally, Grinburg said, "But, sir, is it a good idea to kill a cop? Mr. Kaplan already said that it is probably bad for business?"

Rabinovich said, "It's also bad for business if people aren't scared of us. In particular, the other mobs, Italians, Jamaicans, Ukrainians, and the rest, have to fear us, or they will try to take over our territory. One of the reasons we have such power in the Philly area is that the others worry about our willingness to exact revenge. But if this cop gets away with no retribution twice, where she involves herself in our business, we look weak, and I will not allow us to look weak!"

Grinburg and Moskowitz looked at each other, unsure that this wouldn't blow up in their faces. But they also knew they had no choice, so all they could do was develop a solid plan and execute it.

And they knew that if their strategy went according to plan, there would be one less cop and one less professor in Philadelphia by tomorrow night!

# Chapter Thirty-Two

Sharon had already left for work very early. She wanted to get in to talk to the captain to see how much she could get for support. She had done him a favor of late, so she knew the captain would do what he could, given the budget constraints that all police forces face these days.

I decided to cancel my classes that day. Sharon told me to stay at home and keep the doors locked. I had not slept well, which was not surprising at all, but more importantly, I wanted to spend some time on the Petrovsky and TechSounds cases. Since I have now been threatened, I knew more was at stake than I had thought.

I now knew that Petrovsky was absolutely involved with money laundering. I had indeed thought that was the case from the info I got from Mikayla at FinCEN, but obviously, there is no doubt at all anymore. I needed to nail down this issue with TechSounds, and how that fits into the overall scheme.

I pulled out all my information about TechSounds and spread it all out in the dining room. There was nothing that jumped out at me at first glance. It looked like just two college guys tried to figure out a way to make money with music, and they were fortunate to have a Deadhead investor who capitalized a million bucks into their venture. Unusual, but certainly not unheard of. But how did Petrovsky Markets and the mob come into play?

Then I suddenly had an idea! Cryptocurrency! That is one of the easiest ways to move money around with little or no trace of the transactions. And because of the Covid pandemic, it had become more challenging to carry cash around physically, so many illegal transactions started to use cryptocurrency and the deep web.

The question was: Why didn't the cryptocurrency action show up on the TechSounds financial statements? Seeing those transactions posted on their financial statements should be pretty straightforward, but they were buried somewhere. Also, I doubt the angel investor, Flannigan, or the two computer nerds would be involved in illegal transactions. But I returned to Brownstein and Williams! I was sure they violated numerous accounting standards, but I wasn't sure how cryptocurrency was in play. Since this was a bit puzzling, I was delighted that I had already contacted Mikayla at FinCEN. She has many more resources at her disposal than I do, and maybe she would be able to help. I decided that I would give her a call later that afternoon.

Meanwhile, Sharon had already set up an appointment in a half-hour to meet with her captain, Frank Russo, to see if he would release a uniform or two to help protect Ben. While she had some time, she decided to contact Sam Bernstein.

She called him, and he picked up on the second ring. "Bernstein."

"Sam, it's Sharon Levin. I'm calling to tell you that a couple of tough guys showed up at Ben's house last night. They were threatening Ben to back off on an accounting investigation that he's involved with."

"Is he okay?"

"Yeah, I showed up just in time and chased the guys off. They got away, but they had some heavy Eastern European accents, so we're thinking Russian or Ukrainian. And while we have no evidence to support this theory, somehow, we both think that our two cases, including the Jewish get one, are somehow related. It's just a feeling for both of us right now, but you know that we play hunches a lot. They don't always work out, but they sometimes do."

"Sharon, I know you have done very well with some of your hunches, including some crazier ones, so I would never ignore any of your feelings. But I don't know how this changes our plans with the divorce inquiry?"

"Actually, it doesn't. I just wanted to give you a heads-up that there might be more going on. Also, I know you know that Emily

Keen of the FBI is on her way up to Philly to help with the ultra-Orthodox case, but Ben spoke to her, and she's going to see if she can shake loose a little time to help with Ben's case, too."

"More the merrier, I say. Just let me know when you're setting up your sting operation, and I will go to work."

"Thanks, Sam. I've got an appointment with the captain to see if he will offer some uniforms to help guard Ben's house. I'll let you know what he says."

"Cap loves you, Levin, so he'll do you right." With that, he hung up.

Sharon made her way to the captain's office and knocked on the door. She heard, "I'm sure it's you, Levin, so come on in."

Sharon smiled as she walked in. "Thanks for taking the time to talk. I'm sure your dance card is full."

Russo said, "Always time for you since you get us such good press with your crazy-ass cases. I'm guessing this is about the Jewish divorces case?"

"Maybe, but maybe not. Ben was threatened at home by two tough guys over an accounting investigation he's doing."

"Uh, he got threatened over an accounting thing. Doesn't he just add and subtract numbers and piss people off how much they have to pay in taxes?"

"Cap, Ben's a professor, so he doesn't do a lot of tax returns anymore. But he does assist an organization called the Public Company Accounting Oversight Board. PCAOB makes sure that auditors do their jobs correctly. Ben is involved with a case involving Petrovsky Markets over in the Northeast. Ever hear of them?"

"Sharon, I was born, raised, and reared in Northeast Philly. Not many places I haven't heard of. I've never been there; not that hot on some Jewish fishes and the like, but I've seen the stores. Three of them, right?"

"Yes, Sir. Ben thinks there may be money laundering, but he doesn't have it nailed down. But he's close. Anyway, I'm going to stay at Ben's home though I'm there most of the time anyway. Also, I've got an FBI agent, Emily Keen, who will also be around. I'm hoping you might give us a uniform or two to hang around outside

Ben's house at night. Emily and I can take turns sleeping, but it would still be helpful if we have someone outside if anyone tries any funny business at night."

"How long are you asking for? You know budgets are tight."

"I think that if these guys are going to try anything, I think they will make their play soon. These two guys are not the leaders, so whoever is in charge will want this taken care of soon. Maybe set someone up for about a week?"

Russo said, "I can give you five nights. I don't think I can go longer with money tight as it is."

"I'll take five nights, Cap. Anything would help. Can we start tonight?"

"I'll authorize it right now. If you're right that if these guys are Russian or Ukrainian, they will want to move quickly. Good luck, Sharon. Keep me in the loop."

"Thanks again. And yes, I will let you know how it's going."

Sharon felt better that she was providing Ben with the best security she could offer. Now all she had to do was close one or even both of the cases in the next five days. She knew she needed to push the cases pretty hard.

She wasn't sure as far as Ben's case, but she knew what to do with the divorce one. Time to check in with Rabbi Shulman!

# Chapter Thirty-Three

Sharon and I were up early. Again, I didn't get much sleep, but better than the previous night. Sharon is used to this kind of pressure, so she slept well. That's actually a good thing, so at least one of us would be fresh.

She said, "Get any sleep?"

"Better than the night before, but I still woke up a lot. You would think that with some of the crazy shit we've been involved with, I would be used to it better, but still not that used to it."

"Don't worry. You can nap this afternoon. Emily will be here soon, and we will take turns staying with you. Can you cancel your classes for another few days? Tell the students that you're sick or something."

"Already took care of that for today. Only have one class and emailed them a problem set to do to turn in next week. It wasn't on the syllabus, but I did tell them I didn't feel well. Indeed, I don't feel well, but not because of being sick. I am pretty wound up right now."

Sharon put her arms around me and said, "Don't worry, babe. Emily, the uniform cops, and I will not let anything happen to you. I promise."

"Even with all the nutty crime stuff you and I have been involved with, both here and abroad, I've always trusted that you'll make sure neither of us gets hurt. But I will admit that having Emily and the uniforms helps with the anxiety level."

At that moment, there was a knock at my door. Sharon put her hand on her weapon and looked out the peephole. She saw Emily holding a small bag, and she opened the door.

Sharon shook hands with Emily and said, "Wow, Emily, you got an early start. Great that you got here so fast."

"I got to bed early last night, so I was up at dawn. Figured I might as well get started." Emily extended her hand, and she and I shook. "Good to see you again, Ben."

"Emily, it's great to see you again, but I wish it were in better circumstances. Thanks so much for helping us out."

"Happy to help. What's an update?"

Sharon said, "We had two uniforms outside overnight. We've got four more nights, but I'm sure if I can show the captain any progress, he'll probably extend us a few more nights."

"I didn't book a hotel room yet because I wasn't sure where you needed me," said Emily.

I replied, "I've got an extra bedroom, and I would be happy for you to use it. It's a queen-size one, and I think you would be comfortable."

Emily smiled and said, "Sleepover! Nice! Don't get to do that very often."

Sharon said, "Yep, we can take turns on watch. I know the uniforms will be there at night, but I would still be more comfortable if we had someone inside awake at night."

"I would certainly agree with that," said Emily. "No reason to take any unnecessary risks. From what you've said, those guys are pretty motivated, so let's be extra safe."

I said, "Wow, having two good-looking women as my bodyguards is quite the treat. Maybe all this craziness is worth it." Both women laughed.

While we were discussing our plan, Grinburg and Moskowitz were discussing their plan. Grinburg said, "So that bosses want us to take care of this tonight. We'll have to break in and then go in guns a blazing. We both have silencers. You ready for this?"

"Gotta be ready. The bosses are disappointed already, so we can't come up short again. Why don't we try to get some sleep in the early evening, and we will be fresh for finishing this off."

"Good idea. Let's crash from 9 to 2, and then we'll be ready for action. Have to figure that the cop and the accountant will be sleeping. Take care of business and head out the door."

Back at my house, Emily stayed with me while Sharon went into the office to try to contact Rabbi Shulman. His office said he was pretty busy today, but she might be able to find some time tomorrow morning. Sharon was disappointed but said she would be in touch early.

Emily and I looked through some of the Brownstein documents, but we didn't see anything that jumped out at us, so we just decided to chat about some compelling cases. Emily knew a little about the Malta, Belgium, and Finland cases, but as I told her more, she found the whole thing fascinating.

Sharon got home at about 6 pm. We told Emily it was her choice for dinner, and she decided to try some Dim Sum over from over on Race Street. We loaded up on a lot of dumplings and some chicken on a stick. Had Door Dash bring everything over. The two uniforms were at their station, and we even offered them some Dim Sum, which they gladly accepted. We thanked them profusely for helping secure my house. Just part of the job said the two cops.

We watched a little TV together and then we decided to crash. Emily took the first shift, and Sharon would relieve her in 3 hours. Emily and Sharon had been on stakeouts enough that they could fall asleep on command.

Grinburg and Moskowitz got up at about 2 am, checked that all their armament was ready, and headed to my house. They rode around the neighborhood and saw the uniforms sitting in their squad car. Grinburg said, "This sucks that there are coppers out there. That's going to make it more difficult. But I don't want to be the one to tell the bosses that we didn't get it done."

Moskowitz replied, "Park on the other side of the block. We'll see if we can come in a back way."

They found a space on Chestnut Street and parked. They made their way through to the back of my house. I had a sturdy lock on the back door, but the mobsters had a crowbar and a metal cutter to open the door. They got their guns with the silencers ready to use.

They quietly tried to open the door and enter. Just as they took their first steps into my house, Sharon, with Emily next to her, pointed her gun right at Grinburg and Moskowitz.

Sharon said, "Nice to see you, boys, again. Why don't you drop your weapons and I'll have the uniforms out front take you two into custody? And please don't try anything stupid because I would love to put a couple of holes in your chests."

Emily said, "If they try anything, can I just shoot the one on the left, and you take the one on the right?"

"Deal!!"

# Chapter Thirty-Four

Once the cops arrested our two intruders, we decided to try to sleep some more, but the ladies still took turns being on watch. We figured that there wouldn't be any more efforts right now, but again,

Sharon decided to err on the side of caution.

All three of us were up by 8 am. I made the coffee and offered food, but no one was hungry. We had put a pretty big dent in the Dim Sum, so no one had much of an appetite. Plus, being attacked by two mob guys also hindered our desire for food.

Sharon said, "Emily, I appreciated your help last night. Since you were on watch, you got me up quickly, and we were ready for our two interlopers."

"Not a problem," replied Emily. "I heard them banging at the door, so I knew something was up. At first, I wanted to let the uniforms out front know, but I thought that might take a little time, so I decided you and I should take control. I figured we had the upper hand between the two of us, our guns and us having the element of surprise. I called the uniforms, and they were there in a flash. We had them under lock and key in about five minutes. No one was in any sort of danger."

Sharon smiled and said, "And I moved so quickly that Ben didn't even wake up until he heard us telling the intruders to drop their weapons."

"Glad we were able to head those guys off. And Ben was right that his extra bed is very comfortable," and she smiled.

"I help where I can," I laughed.

Emily asked, "So what's the next thing on the agenda? Time to head into the precinct to interrogate those two idiots?"

"That's the plan. I think my captain even wants to get involved with this one. What are you have on your plate?"

Emily said, "Well, I was supposed to be helping you with the Jewish case, and since we haven't finished that one, my boss said I should stick around for a few days. You want me to move out to a hotel now?"

I said, "Absolutely not! You helped protect me, so the least we can do is put you up for a few days. Plus, if your boss doesn't have to pay for your housing, maybe you can stick around a little longer. I'm assuming that the FBI, like the Philly police force, likes it when you keep costs down if possible."

"That's for sure. If it's okay with you two, I'll refresh my memory on the Jewish divorce case while Sharon takes the statements from those two mobsters. They will not say much if they are any like the other mob assassins I've worked with. If they give up any important information, the bosses of their mob group will ensure the two are not in good health, if not dead. Even to the FBI, it is somewhat amazing who the mob can get to if they want to harm someone."

Sharon said, "Isn't that the truth? And I agree that the two will not give up much info, but we must go through the process. Once I'm done with those two, I'll come back here so we can work on the divorce case. As I said, I don't think anyone else will return for Ben now, but better safe than sorry, at least for a few days."

While Sharon was heading out to the precinct and Emily and I were looking at some Jewish divorce info, Mikhail, Boris, and Leonid huddled at their office to figure out what to do next. All three were hopping mad.

Mikhail roared, "I can't believe those dumbasses let themselves get caught! They almost got caught the first time, and they should have taken better care before they tried again. And Grinburg had the guts to use his phone call to ask if we would send him a lawyer. What are we: Part of their new legal team or something?" We pay them very well to care for our problems, and they didn't do that in this case."

"To be honest, Mikhail," added Boris, "I think they felt they were under a lot of pressure from us to make the accountant and the lady cop disappear. I'm not defending them, but I understand why they thought they needed to move quickly. Plus, getting them an attorney will bide us some time to figure out what to do next."

Leonid said, "It doesn't matter whether it was a good move; it's done. The question is, what are we going to do now?"

"I'm not worried about what those two idiots will say," said Mikhail. "They know that if they give up any important information, they're dead men. They know that their bosses can get to anybody, anytime. But we need to figure out what we're going to do now."

Boris suggested, "Obviously, we're going to lay low for a while. It's clear that between the divorce work and the accounting search, the cops are looking at us on two fronts. We must step back for a while and let things cool down."

"But we still need to conduct some business," said Mikhail. "In fact, we haven't even been paid the second installment of $75,000 for the additional get that we got for that guy, Isak. It's due tomorrow, and I still want to get paid. All he has to do is show up with the money. There's not any risk in just getting paid, is there?"

Boris replied, "Probably not. I'm going to contact Isak and tell him it's time to pay up. Once we have that in hand, we'll keep a low profile for a while, and things will smooth over."

The mob guys didn't know that Sharon and Emily were putting together the sting operation. Meanwhile, I was going to check in with Mikayla at FinCEN to see if I could find any link between the two cases. The sting operation was not on my schedule of events, but I needed to keep busy. Idle hands and the like!

# Chapter Thirty-Five

Sharon's captain allowed her to question the two who broke into my house. They had been given a sleazy lawyer the captain knew from other shady characters, and he knew the guy was scum. All the lawyer said was that his clients were pleading the fifth on everything. Wasn't that much to talk about, so the two were returned to their cells, and the lawyer left.

Sharon decided to check in with Rabbi Shulman. He picked up on the second ring: "Rabbi Shulman."

"Rabbi, this is Detective Sharon Levin. I wanted to follow up with what happened with the guy, David, I think is his name, and whether you still feel like you want to help us find out what has been happening in the ultra-Orthodox community."

"Detective, I have given it some thought, and yes, I think I will assist you in any way I can. If these shakedown artists are causing bodily harm to force men to sign a get, then that needs to be stopped. How can I help?"

"Well, the first thing to find out about is whether another father-in-law was the one behind the second assault. Have you spoken to the father-in-law involved?"

Shulman replied, "I have not yet done that, but I have a man in question, Isak Zylberman, coming to my office at 3 pm. Would you like to be included in the questioning?"

"Absolutely! I will meet you at your shul by 2:30 pm. I also want to thank you for all your assistance."

"As I said, if these men did what you suggested, it's an abomination to our religion, and they have to be held accountable."

"Rabbi, that is just what I want to hear. See you this afternoon."

Sharon felt good that the rabbi was willing to help. She thought the rabbi could move this investigation along, and if her theory was correct, the rabbi's assistance was vital.

Sharon decided to check in with Bernstein. She called his number, and he picked up on the first ring. "Bernstein."

"Sam, it's Sharon. I've got an appointment with Rabbi Shulman at 3 pm to meet with the father-in-law, who might be behind the second assault. I think that if this guy, Isak Zylberman, is behind the second attempt, we may need the rabbi to help set up the sting. Can you come to my office and talk about how that might work?"

"On my way up with the bad coffee."

Bernstein said, "Sounds like you've made some progress. By the way, I heard about last night. Nice job protecting your accounting buddy."

"Thanks. I had help from the FBI, but we did okay last night."

"I think you did better than okay. Am I correct that the two guys you caught just lawyered up and are saying nothing?"

"You got it," said Sharon. "Still not sure my, or even now our case, is related to Ben's, but it's looking more and more like they are linked. If there are mob bosses involved with both cases, they will go to the ground because we caught those two last night. We need to move quickly."

"Completely agree! Want me to come with you to meet the rabbi? We need to figure out how we can connect the dots."

"That would be great. The rabbi already expects me, but I doubt he will also object to your being there. Got any ideas on how to play it?"

Sam said, "Gotta believe that if this Isak is involved, he probably owes the mob some money. Doubt they have had time to settle up already. If we can put me in play with the mobsters, we can set up a wiretap. Isak could wear a wire, but I doubt he can keep himself together while facing the mob. We need to figure out how to get me to replace him."

"I'll give it some thought, you do the same, and we'll talk about it on the way over to the shul."

"See you in a little while."

Sharon continued to thumb through what she had on the divorce case. She knew she needed to contact a ringleader or two with the mob. But much of it hinged on what this guy, Zylberman, would be willing and able to do. It all depended on how complex the rabbi was ready to push him.

Sharon and Bernstein met at 2:30 pm and headed to the synagogue. They tried out some ideas, but they agreed that if this father was indeed involved, it all depended on what the rabbi would do.

Sharon and Sam arrived at the shul at 2:50 pm. Sharon knocked on the door, and Rabbi Shulman opened the door. He said, "Thank you for coming, Detective Levin. It seems you have another guest with you."

Sharon said, "This is Detective Sam Bernstein. He has offered to assist us in this inquiry. I hope it is acceptable to you to have him involved."

"To be honest, Detective, this whole thing is way over my head, so any assistance you or your colleague can offer is gratefully appreciated. Both of you, please come in."

The three sat in the rabbi's office and chatted a little about the weather and the Phillies. Apparently, the rabbi was a huge fan. The rabbi's phone rang, and his assistant told him his appointment had arrived. Shulman went to the door to bring in Isak.

Shulman said, "Isak, I have asked these two police officers to sit in on our discussion. This is Detective Levin and Detective Bernstein."

Isak said in a choked sound, "But, rabbi, I thought you asked me to come in about how my daughter is doing after David filed for a divorce."

"Isak, that is part of it, but the detectives and I have a more important question to ask. I'm not going to waste any time, so I will say it out loud: Did you pay some mobsters to attack David to get him to sign the get?"

"Rabbi, why would you say such a thing," said Isak in a calm voice.

"Because Isak, I find it very unlikely that David decided to sign the get so soon after Lev Brodsky was accosted and killed. We have a few divorces in our community now and then, but two in such a short period is quite unusual, as I'm sure you would agree."

"But it could happen, couldn't it?" asked Isak.

"It could, but I doubt it. So, I will ask you as your rabbi, and I want the truth: Were you involved in an attack on David that convinced him to sign the divorce documents? And don't lie to your rabbi, Isak."

Isak turned his head and slumped down. He sat for over a minute before he did anything. Finally, he said, "Please forgive me, rabbi, but yes, I paid members of the Russian mob to get David to sign the get. I had found out that he had had an affair and that, coupled with his unwillingness to provide an income to my family, angered me to such an extent that I took such a shameless act."

Sharon decided to jump in and asked, "How much were you to pay?"

"The total bill was to be $100,000 with 25 grand up front."

Bernstein interrupted, "And is it that you still owe them the $75,000? Please say yes."

Isak lowered his head again and said, "I just got a call from one of the gangsters demanding that I deliver that amount to them tomorrow."

Bernstein turned to Sharon and smiled, "There's our opening!"

# Chapter Thirty-Six

While Sharon had an obvious idea of what she would do next, I was still bubbling around for my subsequent move. Emily knew a little about accounting and certainly a lot about money laundering, but we didn't have a precise angle to make a move.

Emily said, "Why don't you contact Mikayla at FinCEN? You and I are a bit stuck, and maybe she can jumpstart where we need to go."

"Good idea," I called Mikayla, and she picked up on the second ring. "Mikayla Heston."

"Mikayla, it's Ben Stone. I've got Emily Keen of the FBI on my speaker phone. I just wanted to update you on what has been happening in Philly these days. Had a little drama."

Emily said, "Hi, Mikayla. Great to hear your voice."

"Emily, it's great to hear you. So, what happened in the drama of Ben's and Sharon's lives? They always are exciting!"

I said, "Well, I had two hoodlums try to break into my house. It's two guys who had threatened me about Petrovsky and TechSounds. Fortunately, Emily and Sharon were ready for their attack, so the two schmucks were easily apprehended. They are under arrest, and Sharon is returning to the Jewish case for now. Emily and I have returned to Petrovsky, TechSounds, and the accounting firm."

"Never a dull moment with you two. Glad Emily was around to help Sharon out. What can I help to help you two?"

I replied, "Well, my new angle is about cryptocurrency and using it for money laundering. I've been racking my brain on how money has been moved around, but the currency has been harder to move because of Covid. I was just wondering if you think you could find out anything about cryptocurrency?"

"Interesting that you brought that up. FinCEN just got an update on the use of cryptocurrency and ransomware. The biggest thing we were told was that even with all the ways similar organizations and we worldwide have tried to combat ransomware, it's still exploding worldwide."

Ransomware! I had never put it together. That's why the numbers haven't been adding up. Petrovsky and the rest have moved away from currency, as I usually think of it, and a lot of it is electronic.

I said, "Mikayla, I never thought of that. I had just moved to cryptocurrency but didn't have the ransomware variable in play. Do you think you can do a little investigating on whether there is any ransomware at play with my case?"

"Already on it. I was going to get in touch today or tomorrow. Based on what you told me, I started digging and found that Petrovsky and TechSounds have the earmarks for cryptocurrency and ransomware. I don't have it all nailed down yet, but I'm sure cryptocurrency and ransomware are in play. The use of crypto is why your numbers haven't been adding up like you would like them to."

I smiled and said, "Mikayla, that is fantastic. And I think finding crypto money in play makes a lot of sense, including the ransomware angle. It's also why the numbers I saw during my audit didn't reconcile. I think the Russian mob has been using Petrovsky and TechSounds to set up ransomware accounts.

Mikayla said, "Now that we are focusing on crypto and ransomware, I have a few tech guys who know their way around crypto, and I'll get them in play today. If there is any link between Petrovsky and the accounting firm using crypto, these two guys can likely find it in a hurry."

I replied, "Mikayla, you are the best. Emily and I will continue trying to dig around on our end, but you have given us a fighting chance to solve this. I really appreciate your help!"

"No problem. I'll be in touch as I have something."

Emily and I sat back and smiled at each other. She said, "Well, Dr. Stone, you might have found that big breakthrough you were waiting for."

"I hope that you are right. But I need your opinion on something. Sharon and I both feel that these two investigations are somehow linked. We don't have it completely locked in, but for some reason, we both feel like we want to play a hunch and see where it leads. What do you think?"

"I firmly believe in following hunches, too. Hell, we were sort of playing a hunch down at the Outer Banks, so I think hunches can provide a significant value to an inquiry. Why do you think these two cases are related?"

I responded, "Well, my case is looking at whether money laundering is happening through the Russian food markets, the music business, and the accounting firm. Sharon believes that the Russian mob is involved with the Jewish divorce business. There is plenty of Russian mob going around in Philly, so it doesn't mean that the cases are related, but she does have a hunch because of how the rabbi has been acting. Also, she has noticed how the first father-in-law, the one whose son-in-law was murdered, seemed almost thrilled that the son-in-law was gone."

Just as I said that, my phone rang for Sharon. I picked it up and said, "So, how is the best-looking murder detective in Philly doing today?"

Sharon laughed a bit and said, "I don't know about the best-looking stuff, but I just found out how I can pull off a sting operation to bring down the guys who are part of the Prodfather gang. I got one of the fathers who paid for the mob guys to threaten a Jewish fella to admit what he had done. The rabbi put the squeeze on him, and that helped. The father still owes the mob $75,000, and they want it tomorrow. I will use one of my fellow officers to stand in and try to get something on tape. I don't know if you've met Sam Bernstein, but he's a very talented cop, and he's not worried about taking a chance to get these mob guys. We'll set it up for tomorrow afternoon, so I hope we can wrap this case up pretty soon. What's going on in your investigative world?"

"I've got cryptocurrency and ransomware on the table right now. Mikayla from FinCEN is putting some of her tech folks looking into how crypto and ransomware might explain why some of the accounting figures I've been seeing don't make sense. She thinks she might get some info later this afternoon or in the morning."

"Sounds like we're both pretty busy, right? But we still have to eat. I assume Emily is still around. Why don't I bring Sam with me, he has been cleared by his wife to do so, and the four of us will have a nice dinner downtown. We haven't wrapped these cases, but we have made much progress. We were not quite ready for a victory lap, but we could at least stretch our legs, hoping that the next lap could come."

"It sounds like a good plan to me. As the overpaid academic, I'll even pick up the tab."

Sharon snickered and said, "Anytime an underpaid law enforcement professional has someone else pay the bill, we consider that a good day at the office. Sam and I will get down to your house in about thirty minutes, and we'll figure out where to go eat."

All four of us knew that tomorrow would be a big day for everyone. A lot of pieces needed to come together, and there would be a lot of stress for all of us. We all deserved a good meal and a lot of drinks!

# Chapter Thirty-Seven

The first thing of the day was that Isak made a call to the Russian racketeers. He was calling from the precinct. Unsurprisingly, he was terrified, but Rabbi Shulman had almost forced him into compliance.

Isak was on the phone with Boris. Isak said, "I am sorry, but I have not yet been able to put together the $75,000 I owe. I told you that I am not a wealthy man, so it has been difficult to garner the necessary funds."

Boris replied, "As we told you, we don't care how you arrange to get the money; you have to get it. We're very unhappy, and I'll tell you right now that having us unhappy is not good for your health. Find the money however it takes."

Isak quietly replied, "As I told you, I don't have the money, but I know someone who can put together that much money. He told me he will front me the $75K so you can get paid."

Boris asked, "Who is this guy?"

"He is a man who offers loans to people in the neighborhood."

Boris knew that meant someone who is a shylock man. Lends money at very steep interest rates. But it wasn't Boris's problem about the shylock. He just wanted the $75 grand. Boris said, "So, who is this guy?"

"His name is Sam Bernstein. He has been lending money in the neighborhood for many years. However, he wants to deliver the money to you personally."

Boris thought, "Not interested. We only deal with you."

"But, sir, Bernstein was emphatic that he needs to deliver the money himself. He said he wants to discuss some other business opportunities with you and your colleagues. He said he felt like you and them could venture into some very profitable arrangements."

Boris knew this was another shakedown artist who wanted to get into business with the Russians. He knew they could just cast him aside after getting the cash they were owed. He said, "Okay, fine. You know where our office is, so tell this man where we are. I expect this guy to deliver the cash by 3 pm."

"Yes, sir. I'm sure Mr. Bernstein can have the money there by then." With that, Isak hung up. He told Sharon and Sam, "They expect the money to be at their office by 3 pm."

Sharon said, "Well, while you were busy on the phone, I got the captain to authorize $75,000 to use in this sting. We will set Sam up with a wire to capture everything said. We've got new types of wires that are not as easily found if these guys try to search Sam. And you gave us the address. By the way, Isak, you are doing the right thing."

Isak said, "Don't have much of choice. I wasn't lying that I don't have all the money."

"Not your problem anymore," said Sam. "We'll take it from here."

Sharon and Sam met with the tech guys to set up the wire. New technology was now available to hide the wire under Sam's shoes. Unless these mobsters were willing to take off Sam's shoes, which was unlikely, they would not find the wire. Then they met with the captain to withdraw the money. The captain said that he expected it to work, or Sharon and Sam would have to pay it back in installments. They both smiled, but they weren't 100% sure that the captain wasn't serious.

At 2 pm, Sam headed out to meet with the gangsters. Sharon and two uniform cops had already set up at the office. Sam pulled into the parking lot where the office was. He decided to go in a little early. Maybe catch them off-guard a bit.

He knocked on the door. He heard a lock being turned, and then the door opened. A guy motioned for him to go inside. When Sam stepped in, the door was closed.

The guy at the door had a gun in his hand. He said, "Put the bag you're holding on the ground. Then spread your arms up so we can frisk you."

Sam had expected this, so he was ready. He dropped the bag and held his hands up. The guy ran his hands over Sam's arms, legs, chest, and most of his body. But thank goodness he didn't check Sam's shoes. That was good because Sharon could hear everything they were saying quite well.

After the fellow finished his pat down of Sam, he told him to pick up the bag and follow him. They went inside, where there was a chair and a few tables. The first guy pointed at Sam to sit down. He asked Sam his name. Sam said, "I think you already know my name is Sam Bernstein. What is your name?"

Boris replied, "My associates and I's names don't matter. But what the hell, I'm Boris, and they are Mikhail and Leonid. Just give us the money you owe, and you can get out of here."

Sam said, "I've got your money right here, but I want to discuss a couple of business opportunities with you."

Mikhail said, "We have plenty of business opportunities, and we don't need any new partners. Just drop the money and leave."

"Aren't you even remotely interested in picking up $200,000 for almost no effort?"

Boris said, "You've got five minutes. Talk fast."

Sam said, "Well, first of all, I know from Isak about the divorces you obtained for some men. I know several men who would also like to get divorced and are willing to pay handsomely for those gets. Also, you may know about several Jewish markets in the area named Petrovsky. I understand that the Petrovsky stores have some connections that can help move money around. I think they are using some cryptocurrency used to clean some of their money. Finally, I've heard there is an accounting firm that can help prevent any financial issues.

All three Russians laughed loudly. Leonid said, "That was a complete waste of time. We already know about those opportunities, so you aren't telling us anything new. So, you need to leave right now!"

Sam stalled a bit by saying, "Gentlemen, I can move a lot of money around that needs to be cleaned. If you gentlemen can assist me in laundering some of my efforts, I can certainly make it worth your while."

"How much worth it?" asked Boris.

"I can cut you in at 20 percent of what I move. As I said, I can start at a million, and you get cut in at $200,000."

And Mikhail said, "And why would we trust you?"

"Because I just handed you a bag filled with $75,000. Let's just say that's a good-faith effort on my part. Isak didn't have the money, and he will have to pay me, but you are getting your dough. That should tell you I am serious about investing with you."

Boris, Mikhail, and Leonid exchanged glances. Finally, Boris said, "I don't think we are ready to invest with you right now, but we may keep you useful for some future investing."

Sam said, "Naturally, I am disappointed about your lack of enthusiasm for the time being, but I hope you will keep me in mind for later. However, I want to ask you one thing before I leave."

Mikhail asked, "What do you want to know?"

"Did it hurt to use a taser on those two guys to encourage them to sign the divorce decrees?"

Leonid smiled and said, "No idea how much it hurt. We had two of our soldiers do the tasing. We try not to get our hands dirty with anything other than money, and even we try to keep clean."

"Well, I hope we can do some business in the future," said Sam, and he quickly left the building. Once, he was in his car and called Sharon and asked, "Do you think you got enough to get a warrant?"

"I'm already on the phone with a judge listening to the tape. I think he's signing the warrant as we speak."

"Then I think we can take them between you, me, and the two uniforms. Just don't want them to get away."

Sharon said, "Not a problem. Judge just signed the warrant and emailed me a copy. Let's bring them in."

Sam smiled and said, "It's like The-A-Team. I love it when a plan comes together."

# Chapter Thirty-Eight

Sharon called me to say they successfully took the Russian mobsters into custody. They called their lawyer immediately and got one of the best criminal lawyers in town. Since these three guys were further up the food chain, they got better representation. Sharon heard the lawyer tell his clients they would be out by midnight. Sharon was sure that the judge in question might keep them overnight just for the hell of it.

The search warrant for the mobsters' house included looking for documents regarding financial transactions. Sharon and the CSI team went through everything in the area and found some financial records. The records were from Brownstein and Williams and clearly focused on Petrovsky and TechSounds. CSI found some USBs with a lot of data, so they knew they had to go through them. Sharon told me about them, and I said if they needed help, I could get Mikayla at FinCEN to use some of their programs. It was late, so there wasn't anything to do right now, but I could try Mikayla in the morning.

Since it was very late, and Sharon had had a very long day, Emily, Sharon, and I just got takeout Chinese and hit the bed. All three of us knew we still had a lot to do tomorrow.

Not surprisingly, Sharon and Emily were up early. Sharon wanted to get to the station before the three Russians were released on bail. She figured she had until noon. Emily had called her boss to tell him about finding out that the Prodfather was true and that two men had been paid to force ultra-Orthodox men to sign divorce decrees. She told her boss that even documents unearthed at the mobs' office illustrated that they were involved with the guy who got killed. It didn't look like any of the top three guys did the killing and torturing, but the three were the ones in charge. Between the Prodfather, the cryptocurrency, and the ransomware, she felt the FBI had a good chance of going after some racketeering charges. Emily's boss was delighted that she had been so successful and told her to stick around for a day to see if any other evidence needed to come back with her to D.C.

I got up later and found out that the CSI wanted to have FinCEN get copies of the USB drives to examine them. I called Mikayla, and she said CSI should just email them what's on the USB drives. Her systems, like the CSI system, could handle large amounts of information. I gave the CSI folks the email address for Mikayla.

It didn't take long for Mikayla and FinCEN to discover that Brownstein and Williams had been moving money around with cryptocurrency. She uncovered that the money from Petrovsky was straight up laundering mob money. Then she found that TechSounds was involved because Flannigan was also moving money around using cryptocurrency. Apparently, Flannigan also wanted to protect some of his assets by moving into crypto. It was nice to find out that the college students didn't know what Flannigan was doing was wrong. They just tried to keep growing the business, and they didn't realize how Flannigan and the mob were using TechSounds to funnel money.

Even though everything was moving quickly, I was unsure who would be taking down Arnold Brownstein. While I wanted the mob guys to go down, having an accounting firm involved with the mob rankled me. Having a CPA partner involved was even worse. I wanted Brownstein to pay for his betrayal of our profession. But I ended up getting what I wanted.

Emily told me her boss had called her to tell her that a warrant had been drawn up for Arnold Brownstein. There were two Philadelphia FBI agents ready to take Brownstein into custody. Emily's boss just wanted to know if she wanted to be included. She responded, "Hell, yes."

Emily and the other two FBI agents entered the offices of Brownstein and Williams. They told the receptionist that they would like to see Arnold Brownstein. At first, the receptionist resisted, but he finally told them that Brownstein was in his office. The three FBI agents just opened the door to Brownstein's office. Emily held up the warrant and said, "Mr. Brownstein, I have an arrest warrant, and I am going to take you into custody."

Brownstein almost looked resigned to this happening. He just stood up and walked behind his desk and held out his hands to be cuffed. As they left his office, Emily said, "By the way. Ben Stone is the reason that this is happening. I just thought you would like to know."

By the end of the day, a lot of things had happened. The two mob guys who had done the killing had found that their bosses had been arrested. The bosses had been released on bail, but their passports were revoked, but that was enough trouble that the two killers started singing like songbirds. They were willing to take their chances since it looked like their bosses were going down, too.

FinCEN also arrested John Flannigan because of the cryptocurrency scheme that he had been doing. He was more than willing to cooperate with FinCEN for fear that he would do a hard time. He was hoping that he would just be fined some money. He would be surprised about how serious FinCEN was about moving money around using crypto. He was going to have more of a penalty than just a fine.

Sharon decided to lobby the District Attorney about letting the two fathers who had funded the Prodfather activities go. She said that both fathers were undoubtedly shunned by their Orthodox community, which would be hard. Also, their daughters will never forgive them for getting one husband killed and another tortured. The DA reluctantly agreed to let them walk.

Sharon, Emily, and I had to debrief when all was said and done that day because so much had happened. I told Sharon to do a recap. She said, "Well, we've got Grinburg and Moskowitz in jail but giving up a lot of information. Boris, Mikhail, and Leonid got out on bail but no passports. They may be the hardest to corral, but the entire police force is on the lookout for them. Plus, the bail was set at $500,000 each, so if they somehow get away, it's still costing them a cool mil. Arnold Brownstein is in FBI custody, but he can probably post bail, too. But whatever does or does not happen legally with Arnold, his accounting practice is done. And Flannigan will also be able to post bail, but FinCEN has him on their radar, so he's not going very far or making any new investment deals. All in all, things worked out pretty well, I would say. Ben, do you still have a bottle of Dom Perignon somewhere hidden in the fridge?"

I said, "Actually, yes, I do. And I certainly think that we all deserve it. Should we call Sam and see if he can come over to join us?"

"I know that Sam is already celebrating with his wife. Why don't we three share this champagne right now? And just so you know, I would like to have everyone involved in these two cases over here. We need food, drink, and a lot of conversation. We'll even try to Zoom in Mikayla if she can't come.

"I'll break open the bubbly."

# Chapter Thirty-Nine

Sharon set up everything to have quite the soiree that night. She had already picked out the food and drink. She bought some delicious steaks that I would be in charge of grilling. Nice potatoes and plentiful vegetables. Key Lime pie for dessert. Also, three bottles of expensive Merlot were included. She invited Rabbi Shulman and picked up a kosher steak to meet his dietary needs.

She had decided on 7 pm because Mikayla took part of the day off so that she could make it down, too. Everyone started to arrive at about six. Emily was still there. Sam Bernstein and his wife, Linda, got there at 6. Rabbi Shulman came next. Mikayla got there at about the same time as the rabbi. And in doing something Sharon seldom did, she included her captain on the invitation list, and very surprisingly, he agreed to come. We had quite the turnout!

I started the steaks at 6:45 pm. We had already set out the dining room table. It was a bit crowded, but we made it work. Sharon had already made the potatoes and veggies, and she had opened the Merlot to let it "breath."

After I got the steaks ready, we all sat down to the feast. It had been quite a while since Sharon and I celebrated, with our collaborators, finishing a case, and we had resolved two cases. We all knew that the three mobsters were unlikely to go to jail, but we still had an impact on them. We were sure they wouldn't be involved with torturing or killing any Jewish men to get them to sign a get. The Philly Prodfather was done.

We got the talk about the cases out of the way first. Everyone offered their take on the cases and how they felt about them. Then we changed the conversation to a wide array of topics. Emily talked about how she decided to join the FBI. Mikayla shared how she had been in public accounting like I was, but she decided that she wanted to join law enforcement and thus FinCEN. Sam cared little about business and was much more interested in the Phillies and the Eagles. Rabbi Shulman decided to talk about going to Israel, which none of us had done. The captain just said that he was enjoying hearing all the stories. And finally, Sharon and I had quite a several choices of stories to tell, but we decided on the female serial killer in Finland. Some attendees had already heard some of the story, but Sharon went into great depth on how it all transpired. Since Rabbi Shulman was the only person not affiliated with law enforcement, he had a lot of questions. After we enlightened him, he said he was glad he had decided to be a rabbi.

The conversation and drink went on until almost 11 pm. Emily was staying at my house for one more night. Mikayla was initially going to stay over, but she decided she needed to return to New York even though it was late. Everyone thanked us profusely for having us over, and people began to depart.

Emily started to want to clean up the dining room and the kitchen, but Sharon was emphatic that the dishes could wait. She said I don't have any classes tomorrow so that I can do the cleaning. I didn't have any classes, so it was hard to argue with her. Emily then decided to crash because she would get up early tomorrow to head back to DC.

I had made some coffee, and Sharon and I decided to sit in the living room for a few minutes. We just leaned back and relaxed and sipped our coffee.

Sharon said, "That was a great dinner, Dr. Stone. Nice job with the steaks!"

"Nice job with everything else, Detective Levin. I think all had a good time."

"I would definitely agree."

As we just sat there and leaned back, I decided to broach what I had decided was the elephant in the room. "So, I just wanted to tell you that I have been thinking about our relationship and where we are."

"Uh oh, are you going to break up with me?"

"Actually, just the opposite. I have been wondering what our next step should be?"

Sharon smiled and said, "And have you arrived at any conclusions?"

"I'm not sure about conclusions, but I've been some pondering. First, you should know this already, but I love you very much."

"I feel the same way about you. I have been for many years. But what do you think should be the next step?"

"That's what's hard. Naturally, the next step is to get married, but I don't know how you feel about that?"

"I've given it some thought, too, but I have also not arrived at any decisions either. To be honest, I feel so strongly about our relationship that it's almost that I don't think we need to be married. In my mind getting married is mostly for other people, not us. Our love is so deep that marriage is almost not necessary."

"How about kids?"

Sharon replied, "That one is a bit tougher. I'll admit that I have thought about kids, but I come from a large family, so I don't feel any pressure to expand the family just for the sake of doing it. How do you feel? You don't have siblings, so you could feel more of a burden to add to the Stone family."

"Indeed, I haven't expanded the family tree directly, but there are many members of the Stone family. My parents only had me, but my dad's brothers had six kids, so many cousins are floating around North Carolina. I don't keep in touch that much, but they are still around. The Stone name is safe without my assistance."

"Ben, I also have to say that the nature of my job makes having kids a little more complicated. I have never been badly injured doing my job, but the fact still exists that my job does entail some risk. I have no intention of getting killed or maimed doing my job, but there is still some peril in my work. Most of the cops in my precinct have kids, and they don't seem to worry about the dangerous aspects of our jobs, but I do."

"I think that is prudent on your part. But, if we're not going to get married and have kids, what can we do to move our relationship to another level?"

"Should I sell my house and move in with you? We've always assumed we would keep separate places, but maybe that was because we weren't ready to say we are in this for the long haul."

I thought for a minute and said, "I've never really thought it that way, but you may be right. Maybe we always knew that if we wanted to break up, all you had to do was move back to your place full-time. Maybe that was our way to protect ourselves from taking the next step."

"So, do you think I should sell my house in South Philly? I'm always here, so it's not that big of a change."

"Yeah, but it does seem to say to me that our relationship is blossoming some."

"Blossoming? That's an interesting choice of words."

I said, "You're right. That's a weird word to use. How about just growing and becoming stronger? Basically, I would like to think that we're not just in a holding pattern. Don't get me wrong, it's a great holding pattern, but I just want more."

Sharon leaned forward and kissed me on the mouth. She said, "I want more, too, and think this is a great idea. Should I go ahead and put my house on the market?"

"Absolutely. Do it as soon as you can. We'll figure out the furniture and the like in your house. What to keep and what to sell or donate. I've got an extra room, but we'll have to make some decisions."

"Sounds like a great plan, Stone. Let's get it started."

I picked out two cocktail glasses, returned to the kitchen, and pulled out a bottle of Smirnoff vodka from the freezer. I poured us each a drink. Then I came back to the living room and handed Sharon a glass.

I took my glass and leaned it forward for us to toast. I said, "Here's to us!"

Thank you for reading.

Please review this book. Reviews
help others find Absolutely Amazing eBooks and
inspire us to keep providing these marvelous tales.
If you would like to be put on our email list
to receive updates on new releases,
contests, and promotions, please go to
AbsolutelyAmazingEbooks.com and sign up.

# About the Author

Steve McMillan has been a management professor for over 25 years but recently turned to writing mysteries. Steve worked in public accounting and real estate before entering academia and uses those experiences coupled with his academic life to develop his stories about accounting and murder. While Steve uses his own life experiences in his character and plot development, he wishes he was as cool as Ben Stone.

For sales, editorial information, subsidiary rights information
or a catalog, please write or phone or e-mail
AbsolutelyAmazingEbooks
Manhanset House
Shelter Island Hts., New York 11965-0342, US
Tel: 212-427-7139
www.AbsolutelyAmazingEbooks.com
bricktower@aol.com
www.IngramContent.com

For sales in the UK and Europe please contact our distributor,
Gazelle Book Services
White Cross Mills
Lancaster, LA1 4XS, UK
Tel: (01524) 68765 Fax: (01524) 63232
email: jacky@gazellebooks.co.uk